S0-AXI-982

A Book of Magic Animals

A BOOK OF
MAGIC
ANIMALS

Ruth Manning-Sanders

ILLUSTRATED BY
ROBIN JACQUES

E. P. Dutton & Co., Inc.   New York

First published in the U.S.A. 1975 by E. P. Dutton & Co., Inc.
Copyright © 1974 by Ruth Manning-Sanders

All rights reserved. No part of this publication may be
reproduced or transmitted in any form or by any means,
electronic or mechanical, including photocopy, recording,
or any information storage and retrieval system now
known or to be invented, without permission in writing
from the publisher, except by a reviewer who wishes to
quote brief passages in connection with a review written
for inclusion in a magazine, newspaper, or broadcast.

LIBRARY OF CONGRESS CATALOGING IN PUBLICATION DATA

Manning-Sanders, Ruth   A book of magic animals

SUMMARY: Eleven folktales from around the world
featuring animals possessing magical qualities.

1. Fairy tales.   [1. Fairy tales. 2. Folklore]
I. Jacques, Robin, ill.   II. Title.
PZ8.M333Br   398.2'452   74-28306   ISBN 0-525-26935-5

Printed in the U.S.A.   First Edition
10 9 8 7 6 5 4 3 2 1

Contents

For permission to re-tell *The Dolphin* the author wishes to thank Messrs Eugen Diederichs Verlag, Düsseldorf and Köln.

1 · The North-west Wind

Well now, there was a peasant – Fanchin was his name – and he had a little field and a little garden. Come spring time he sowed corn in the field and planted an apple tree in his garden. The corn sprang up; the apple tree blossomed and bore fruit. Fanchin watched the corn grow; he counted the apples on the tree. Come autumn he saw the corn turn golden and the apples turn red. He said to his wife, 'Tomorrow I will cut the corn, and you shall pick the apples.'

But that night came the North-west Wind, roaring and ravaging; and by morning all Fanchin's corn was flat, and his little apple tree was torn up by the roots.

I tell you, Fanchin was mad, he danced with rage. He took a stick and set off to kill the North-west Wind. And if he went fast it was because his rage wouldn't let him go slow; but fast or slow, it was all one, because he didn't know where the North-west Wind lived. He was asking everyone he met, but that wasn't any use, because nobody knew any more than he did.

In the evening he came to an inn, and he had only a few pence in his pocket, so the innkeeper said he could sleep in the stable. And as he was lying down in the straw something gave a heave, and there was a big monkey rubbing the sleep out of his eyes and peering at him.

'Hullo there!' says the monkey.

'Hullo to you!' says Fanchin.

'If it's not too bold a question, what might you be doing here?' says the monkey.

Fanchin tells him. And now Fanchin is raging again about nobody being able to give him a right direction to the North-west

7

Wind's house, when the monkey interrupts. 'Well, I know most things, I do. I know where the North-west Wind lives and all. Could take you there, too, I s'pose. Only it's a tidy step from here, and my legs aren't shaped for long walking. But if you'd give me a heave up on your back now and again, I expect I could manage.'

So Fanchin agreed to do that; and as soon as ever it came dawn, the two of them set out. The monkey went scampering along ahead of Fanchin for a while; but by and by he sat down on the road and said his legs wouldn't carry him another step. So Fanchin heaved him on to his back.

Then it was, 'Gee up, my fine fellow!' with the monkey playing ride-a-cock-horse, bouncing up and down on Fanchin's back, digging his knees into Fanchin's ribs, and taking hold of Fanchin's two ears, making out they were reins. Fanchin wasn't much enjoying it, as you may suppose. All the same he put up with it for a bit; and along and along they went, till they came to a place where three roads met, one straight and the two others twisty. Fanchin was for taking the middle road, which was the straight one; but the monkey was for taking the right-hand twisty one, and he was pulling at Fanchin's right ear.

'Stop it!' says Fanchin.

'Turn right!' says the monkey.

'Straight on's the better road,' says Fanchin.

'Turn right!' says the monkey.

'I won't,' says Fanchin.

So then the monkey set his teeth in Fanchin's right ear, and bit hard.

Fanchin gave a yell, tumbled the monkey off his back, and set about him with his stick. The monkey gave a leap to a tree, broke off a branch and set about Fanchin. So there they were the two of them, jumping round and round, and whacking away at each other and neither winning, till at last Fanchin laughed and said, 'Oh well, have it your own way!' and lifted the monkey on to his back again, and took the road to the right.

That road was soon all a dazzle of light, for it led to the Mountains of Gold. And on a plain beyond the Mountains of Gold stood the

House of the Winds. So Fanchin got there at last, and he strode up to the door, thumped on it, and shouted, 'North-west Wind, North-west Wind, where are you? You who stamped on my corn and flattened it, you who tore up my dear little apple tree – come out, because I'm going to kill you!'

Well, the door flew open with a bang then, and before Fanchin could cry 'Oh!' the North-west Wind had got a grip of him, and was whirling him in the air, right side up, wrong side up, blown about like any scrap of paper in a gale, and he might have been blowing about to this day if the monkey hadn't set his teeth in the North-west Wind's leg and bitten with all his might. So then the North-west Wind put Fanchin down and said, 'Well, I see we'd best be friends. I'm sorry about your corn and your apple tree – it was only my fun. But come into the house and I'll give you a present.'

So Fanchin went into the House of the Winds. All the other winds were asleep in there, lying on golden sofas. Their breathing ruffled Fanchin's hair, and filled the house with a gentle sighing. But they none of them woke, which was a good thing for Fanchin, who was walking on tiptoe and feeling rather nervous. The North-west Wind took him right through the house into a garden at the back, where there was a little apple tree growing in a pot.

'Here you are,' says he to Fanchin. 'Take this little tree home and plant it. It's a magic tree; it will not only give you apples, it will give you anything you ask it. Ask it for something now, and you'll see.'

Well, Fanchin was feeling hungry, so he said, 'Please, little tree, give me something good to eat.'

Did you ever! Immediately the branches of the little tree were hung with fried sausages and pork pies and sweet cakes and bottles of wine. Fanchin and the monkey set to and had a good meal. And when they couldn't eat any more – well, there wasn't any more to eat: only green leaves, and some small tight flower buds which might by and by turn into apples – or into anything else that Fanchin chose to name.

So then all was friendliness. Fanchin thanked the North-west Wind, and, carrying the little apple tree, set off with the monkey

on his journey home. The North-west Wind speeded them on their way by blowing behind them, but only gently, not to upset them. Towards evening they came to the inn, and the innkeeper, who wasn't too pleased to see them again, was about to hand Fanchin the key of the stable, when Fanchin said, 'No, no; supper first,' marched into the parlour, set his little tree on the table and said, 'Little tree, little tree, give us something really good for supper.'

Immediately there was the little tree laden with food again – roast meat and puddings and fruit and wine. The innkeeper gasped and stared. He ran to fetch his wife; his wife gasped and stared. They sat down to supper with Fanchin and the monkey, and both agreed that it was the most delicious meal they had ever had in all their lives.

Well, after that the innkeeper was offering Fanchin his best bedroom, and Fanchin said yes, if the monkey might share it. And the innkeeper even agreed to that. So Fanchin and the monkey were soon lying snug on feathers, and they fell asleep immediately, for they were very tired.

Fanchin, the careless fellow, had left his little tree standing on the parlour table. So what did the innkeeper do? He carried that little tree out into his garden. He took the tree out of its pot and planted it in his orchard. Then he pulled up the smallest of his own apple trees, and having cut it and trimmed it into the shape of Fanchin's little tree, he planted it in Fanchin's pot and set it on the parlour table. He had breakfast ready cooked, too, before Fanchin got up next morning, so Fanchin hadn't to ask the tree for anything. And the long and the short of it was that Fanchin set off home carrying the wrong apple tree. And when he at last got home, and showed his wife the tree, and ordered it to give them a good meal – well, of course, nothing happened.

So back goes Fanchin all the way to the House of the Winds; and the rage he felt before was nothing to the rage he felt now. He went so fast that the monkey had to run to keep up with him; and when he reached the House of the Winds he was stamping and shouting, 'Ah, you rogue of a North-west Wind, come out, come out! Give me back all you have taken from me, or I will thrust my knife into your heart!'

Then the North-west Wind came out of the house; he was laughing, and his laughter set Fanchin and the monkey spinning round like tops. 'Well, well, well,' laughed the North-west Wind, 'lost your little tree, have you? And whose fault is that? Not mine surely! But here's something else for you.'

And he gave Fanchin a little clod of earth.

'This clod,' says he, 'will become a big field, or a little field, or a field of any size you tell it to be. It will also produce any crop you tell it to produce. So be off home with you now, and take better care of my second present than you did of my first.'

Well, off goes Fanchin towards home again, carrying the clod of earth, and with the monkey skipping along beside him. They come to the inn and Fanchin decides to spend the night there. So when suppertime comes – ah, the silly fellow – he takes the clod of earth out of his pocket, lays it on the table and says, 'Now become a little grass field, just the size of this table, and let the first crop you produce be a good supper.'

Immediately, there's the table covered with a growth of short grass, and on the grass a picnic supper laid out. Fanchin and the monkey and the innkeeper and his wife eat and drink, and the innkeeper thinks, 'Ho! Ho! It's easier to steal a clod of earth than to steal an apple tree!' And steal that clod of earth he does; and in the morning, the clod that Fanchin carries home in his pocket is a clod from the innkeeper's back yard. So when Fanchin boasts of it to his wife, and lays it down in front of his house and says, 'Little clod of earth, become a tidy-sized field planted with beans' – well, that clod doesn't become a field of any size, whether big or little.

'The North-west Wind has deceived me again!' yells Fanchin. 'And now I *will* kill him!'

He sets off yet a third time for the House of the Winds. This time he's carrying a pistol; and the first thing he does when he reaches the House of the Winds is to take a shot at the North-west Wind, who was standing in the doorway looking out.

What happened? The shot went clean through the North-west Wind, like going through mist. But the North-west Wind didn't laugh this time: he was very, very angry. He was blowing Fanchin up into the air, and round and round, and letting him fall, *bump*, and blowing him up again. And Fanchin was taking more shots with the pistol, and the shots were all going wide, and both he and the North-west Wind were shouting and swearing; and the monkey, who thought it was his duty to stick up for Fanchin, however foolish Fanchin might be, had scrambled up on to the shoulders of the North-west Wind, and was biting his nose and pulling out his long yellow hair in handfuls.

So at last the North-west Wind had had enough of it, and he called out, 'Fanchin, Fanchin, tell your monkey to leave me alone! If you'll promise never to come here again, I will give you another present, and tell you how to get back your apple tree and your clod of earth.'

So then Fanchin called the monkey off, and put his pistol in his belt, and the North-west Wind went into the House of the Winds and came out again carrying a little box.

'In this box there is a river,' said he. 'You have only to lift the lid and say, "River, river, come out of my box! Drown whom you will, but do not drown me." And the river will come out, and go on flowing, and getting wider and wider, and deeper and deeper, until you order it into the box again. When the innkeeper finds himself up to the chin in water I think he'll be glad enough to give back what he's stolen. And now goodbye to you, Fanchin. And I don't mind if I never see you again,' says he, and goes into the House of the Winds and slams the door.

So, with his little box in his pocket, and the monkey for company, Fanchin set off once more on his way home.

When he came to the inn he was scowling fiercely, and the innkeeper, with his guilty conscience, wasn't too pleased to see him. All the same that innkeeper put a bold face on it, and said, 'Welcome, welcome, friend Fanchin! And has the North-west Wind given you yet another fine present?'

'Yes, indeed he has,' says Fanchin. 'He's given me a little river to drown thieves in. So hand me back my apple tree and my clod of earth, or my river shall begin with you.'

'I don't know what you're talking about,' says the innkeeper.

'I'm talking about my apple tree and my earth clod that you stole from me,' says Fanchin.

'*I* stole! *I*!' says the innkeeper.

'Yes, you,' says Fanchin.

Well, the innkeeper still doesn't know what Fanchin's talking about, and he keeps on not knowing until Fanchin loses his temper, takes the little box out of his pocket, sets it on the ground, lifts the lid and says, 'River, river, come out of your box. Drown whom you will, but do not drown me.'

'Nor me, Fanchin! Nor me!' cries the monkey.

'Nor my monkey of course,' says Fanchin.

So then the water began to trickle out of the box in a little stream, and the little stream became a big stream, and the big stream became a torrent, and the torrent became a raging river: the whole land-scape was going under water, except for a little square of path where Fanchin stood with the monkey, and that was dry and kept on rising above the flood that poured round it. The inn had

13

disappeared under water, except for one chimney; and to that chimney the innkeeper and his wife clung screaming.

'Help, we drown! Help, help, we drown! You shall have back your apple tree, you shall have back your clod of earth! Help, help, help, help! We drown! We drown!'

Then Fanchin told the water to go back into the box; and the raging river shrank to a torrent, and the torrent shrank to a big stream, and the big stream shrank to a little stream; and the little stream shrank to a trickle. The trickle went back into the box, and Fanchin put the lid on the box, and the box in his pocket.

There was the inn now, just as it had been before. The innkeeper and his wife came down from the roof. The innkeeper ran to his garden and dug up Fanchin's little apple tree; he hurried to fetch the clod of earth from the cellar where he had hidden it. He thrust both tree and clod into Fanchin's hands. 'Take them and go!' he cried. 'Take them and go!'

Now all was well. The first thing Fanchin did when he got home was to set the little apple tree on the kitchen table and order it to give himself and his wife and the monkey a good meal. And they got their good meal. So, after that, Fanchin took his clod of earth, set it down in front of his cottage, and said, 'Clod, clod, become a great big garden, full of fruit trees, and flowers and vegetables, and everything beautiful and useful.'

And no sooner were the words out of his mouth, when lo – there was the garden.

Fanchin went down to the bottom of the garden, took his little box out of his pocket, put it on the ground, lifted the lid, and said, 'River, river, come out of your box. Flow gently and brightly, my river, among rushes and willows.'

At once the water began to trickle out of the box in a little stream; and the little stream became a big stream, and the big stream became a bright, gently flowing river, with golden rushes growing on its banks, and willow trees bending over their reflections in its quiet waters.

After that, the days passed pleasantly for Fanchin. When he was tired of working in his wonderful garden, he amused himself by fishing in the river. And the monkey followed him everywhere, carrying his tools, working at his side, and baiting his fish hooks. So one day the monkey said, 'Fanchin, have I been a help to you?'

'Surely you have, my monkey.'

'How many times have I helped you, Fanchin?'

Fanchin considered. 'Well, three big times, and lots and lots of little times – more times than I can count.'

'Then goodbye, Fanchin. You won't see your monkey any more.'

'Oh, oh, my monkey, you're not going to leave us?'

'Yes, your monkey's going to leave you, Fanchin.'

Fanchin was hurt. He had grown very fond of his monkey. He began to grumble. 'I don't see why you need go and do that – just when we've got used to you and all!'

But the monkey laughed, and turned three somersaults: *whizz, whizz whizz,* so fast that Fanchin felt giddy and shut his eyes. And when he opened his eyes again – what did he see? No monkey, but a little laughing boy, without a stitch of clothing on him.

'Oh!' says Fanchin. 'Oh! Who are you?'

'Well,' says the little laughing boy, 'I used to be your monkey, but now I'm your little son – if you'll have me, Fanchin? When I was a baby a fairy found me under a bush, and took me home to live with her. But I was such a naughty, ungrateful boy that she turned me into a monkey. "And a monkey you shall remain," says she, "until you've proved as helpful to someone else as you've been *un*helpful to me." So that's how it's all come about, Fanchin.'

'Well! Think of that!' says Fanchin. 'And my missus and I have always wanted a son!'

So he took the little boy by the hand and went in to tell his wife.

And they were all three very happy.

2 · The Little Humpbacked Horse

I The Firebird

A farmer had three sons. Daniel was the eldest, Gabriel came next, and Jack was the youngest. The farmer sowed many acres of wheat. The wheat sprang up strong and vigorous; but just as the ears began to turn golden there came a thief in the night who tore up the wheat in one place, and trampled it down in another place; but left no footmarks to tell what manner of thief it might be, whether man or beast.

So the farmer said that his sons should take it in turns to guard the fields at night; and that evening he gave Daniel a pitchfork and an axe and a coil of rope, and sent him to the fields. But the night was dark and stormy, and it began to rain. No, Daniel wasn't going to catch his death of cold for any tiresome thief; so he went up into the hayloft over the stables, and there, on a soft bed of hay, he slept peacefully till dawn. Then he jumped up, ran to the water trough in the yard, filled a bucket, soused his head and shoulders, and so, dripping wet, went to bang on the farmhouse door.

'Hey, hey, hey! Open up!'

Gabriel came. 'Well, brother, did you see anything? Did you hear anything? Did you catch the thief?'

And Daniel answered, 'I saw nothing but darkness. I heard nothing but the wind. I caught nothing, unless it be my death of cold. Surely it can be only the wind and the rain that tear up, and trample down, and leave no footmarks of their coming and going.'

'I do not think it is the wind and the rain,' said the farmer.

And next night he sent Gabriel to keep watch.

But Gabriel didn't even trouble to go to the fields. He strolled off to the village, spent the night merrily enough with one or two of his friends, and, returning before cockcrow, came to knock on the farmhouse door.

'Hey, hey, hey! Open up!'

This time the farmer himself opened the door. 'Well, my son, what have you seen? What have you heard?'

'Grey shapes gliding, and hollow voices moaning: they are ghosts that haunt our fields. And against ghosts what can man do?'

'I do not think it can be ghosts,' said the farmer. And that night he sent Jack to watch.

So off goes Jack, with his pitchfork and his axe, and his coil of rope. He sits down behind a holly bush; he keeps himself awake by counting the stars. And yet he was nearly asleep when there came a soft rustling, and a stealthy stepping, and a fragrant breathing – some creature passing by on cautious feet.

Jack jumped up – what did he see? A great white mare with mane and tail of brilliant gold that glittered in the starlight. Now she was in the wheat, trampling down the blades, nibbling off the ears, tossing her gleaming head, moving on, and leaving a trail of ruin behind her.

Jack stood up. Cautiously, on tiptoe, holding his breath, moving without a sound, he crept after the mare: a leap, he had her by the glittering mane, another leap as she swung round, and he was up on her back but, alas, with his face to her tail, and clinging to that tail for dear life, for she was off at a furious gallop, over the fields and on and on, up hill, down dale, kicking up her heels, rearing, bucking, now on her hind legs, now on her forelegs, and Jack scarcely conscious of where he was, or what was happening, but still stubbornly clinging on. Until in her wild gallop she came back into the fields, and stopped beside the holly bush, with such a sudden jerk that Jack slid from her back, and thinking he had lost her, made a grab at her mane.

But she stood quietly, breathing through wide-open nostrils, and said, 'Jack, I own I'm beaten, so now we must part friends. Let me go, and I will give you two horses like myself, so beautiful, so beautiful that their equal has never yet been seen by mortal man. And I will give you also a third horse, a very little one. The first two you may sell; but never, never part with the little one, for you will find him the best friend that ever man had.'

Jack thought. Then he said, 'All right.' And the mare galloped away.

Jack thought again. 'Well there, maybe I've been a fool to let her go.'

No – he hadn't been a fool! For see now, trotting towards him come two most beautiful horses, white like the mare, and like her with manes and tails of purest gold. Tossing their lovely heads, and prancing in their pride, they trot up to stand one on each side of Jack, as if to say, 'At your orders, master!'

But, oh see – what's coming now? A tiny, tiny horse, no bigger than a fox, and like no creature *you* have ever seen, nor I. For he has ears a yard long, and two humps on his back.

Oh ho! Jack takes up his coil of rope, chops off three tidy lengths with his axe, ties up the three horses to the holly bush, and scampers home to bang on the farmhouse door.

The farmer comes to the door. 'Well, son, did you hear anything? Did you see anything?'

'Eh, little father, I caught three horses.'

'Well done, my son! And where are they?'

'Eh, little father, I tied them to a bush. You come and see!'

But the farmer said, 'You are cold, and you must be hungry. First you shall have breakfast, and then you shall take me to see the horses.'

So Jack went into the kitchen to have his breakfast.

Then Daniel winked at Gabriel, and Gabriel nodded at Daniel. They stole out, they fetched two bridles, they ran to the fields. They came to the bush, they untied the two beautiful white horses with golden manes, they bridled them, jumped on their backs, and off at a gallop to sell the horses in the city.

So when Jack, having breakfasted, all joyful, brings his father to the bush in the fields – what does he see there? Only the tiny horse with his two humps and his yard-long ears.

'Oh, oh, oh, someone has stolen my lovely horses! Someone has stolen them!' Jack shed tears, he fairly howled, he cursed the thieves. 'Someone has stolen my lovely horses, my lovely white horses with the golden manes and tails!'

The farmer didn't know what to make of it. He left Jack blubbering and cursing, and went home.

But then little Humpy up and spoke. 'Jack, Jack, this won't do! You are cursing your own brothers, for it is they who have stolen

the golden-maned horses. But quick, Jack, on to my back with you, and we'll soon catch up with the golden manes. When *I* gallop I go swifter than any wind that blows.'

So Jack sat on Humpy's back, between the two humps, and off galloped the little horse, with his long ears streaming out on either side, and Jack glad enough to get a hold of those long ears, for sometimes Humpy was rushing over the ground, and sometimes he was rushing through the air, and the world was whizzing backwards past Jack at such a rate that he had to shut his eyes for very giddiness.

'There they are!' cried Humpy. And Jack, opening his eyes, saw flashes of gold on the road ahead: Daniel and Gabriel galloping fast on the golden-maned horses.

Yes, they were galloping fast, but Humpy was galloping faster. He caught up with Daniel and Gabriel; he took a spring right over their heads, and came down on the road in front of them.

Daniel and Gabriel had to pull up then – they were looking very foolish.

'And who would ever have believed,' cried Jack, 'that brothers would steal a brother's horses!'

'Oh no, brother, not *steal*,' said Daniel. 'We were only taking them to the city to sell for little father – to make up for the loss of the wheat. Don't you agree that little father should be paid for the loss of the wheat?'

Well, Jack was easy going, and Daniel was sly; he talked Jack round, and soon they were all three riding to the city together.

So on they rode, and on they rode, and the sun set, and it was twilight, and then night. There was no moon, the sky was clouded, not a star was showing, and it was very dark: except for the brightness of the golden manes and tails – and that brightness only made the surrounding night more black.

Daniel said, 'Let us halt here under these trees by the side of the road, tether the horses, and wait for dawn.'

Well, they did that, but it was very cold under the trees. Gabriel grumbled. Daniel said, 'See there, see there across the fields – surely a fire burning! If we had a burning brand *we* could make a fire. Jack, be good to us, hurry on your swift little horse, and beg a lighted brand from whoever it is that has one.'

So good-natured Jack loosed Humpy and got on his back. One leap – Humpy was off across the fields. And what did Daniel and Gabriel do then? They untethered the golden-maned horses, and mounted, and galloped away on the road to the city.

Meanwhile, Humpy was carrying Jack across the fields. And the nearer they drew to the fiery light, the bigger and brighter it became, until it seemed to light up the world; every leaf on every tree sparkled, and the grass under Humpy's feet shone emerald.

'That must be the biggest fire ever man made!' said Jack. 'But there seems to be no smoke, and I feel no heat.'

'Because it isn't a fire,' said Humpy. 'It's a feather from a fire-bird's wing. And now that you know what it is, we'd best be turning back.'

'Oh no,' says Jack, 'oh no – I must have that feather!'

Humpy said, 'Leave the feather where it is.'

Jack said, 'No, I must have it!'

And he urged Humpy on to where the feather lay glittering on the grass, picked it up, wrapped it in his handkerchief, and put it in his pocket. Now everything was dark.

'No good will come of this!' said Humpy, and trotted back to the high road.

Well there – Daniel and Gabriel had gone, the golden-maned horses had gone; there was nothing to do but chase after them again. And chase after them Jack and Humpy did, and caught up with them next morning just as they were entering the city, and all rode in together, Jack this time very haughty, and his brothers feeling very foolish, and making excuses which Jack wouldn't listen to.

But they had scarcely entered the city before they were surrounded by a crowd of people, and the crowd grew bigger and bigger as they made their way to the market-place; for such horses as these golden-maned horses had never before been seen in that town or in any other town, and as to little Humpy, he was a show in himself.

And the news came to the Tsar, and the Tsar ordered out his carriage and drove to the market-place; and as soon as he sees those two horses – yes, he must buy them! And who is the owner?

Well, Jack is the owner.

And will Jack sell them?

Well, yes, Jack thinks he will.

And what does Jack want for them?

Well, Jack thinks his hat full of gold would do nicely.

So he gets his hat full of gold, and the Tsar orders four of his grooms to lead away the horses. But the horses won't be led away; they break the reins, kick up their heels, and trot back to Jack. Well then, Jack must lead them to the royal stables, and so he does, and Humpy follows. And Jack, having seen the horses into their stalls, goes off with Humpy to an inn. But first he finds a trusty messenger and sends the gold home to his father, with a scrawled note which says *For little father from the golden-maned horses to pay for the trampled wheat.*

Then of course Jack's brothers, Daniel and Gabriel, come to the inn all smirks and flatterings, hoping for a share of the gold. But Jack shows them his empty hat, and tells them that the gold's gone to little father. So then they sneak off out of the city – and out of the story, too – and a good riddance!

But up in the Tsar's stables the golden-maned horses are moping. They won't eat, they won't drink, they won't be groomed; they kick and bite when the grooms come near them. They grow shaggy, grubby, mere bags of bones, it looks as if they are starving themselves to death – what's to be done?

The Tsar sends for Jack. He is angry, he upbraids Jack for selling him bewitched horses.

Bewitched? Nonsense! Jack goes to the stable. See there! The golden-maned horses whinny their welcome. Now they will eat, now they will drink, now they will stand quiet for Jack to groom them. Well then, that's how it is: if the Tsar would keep the golden-maned horses he must also keep Jack, and if he keeps Jack, he must also keep Humpy.

So now here's Jack, happy with his golden-maned charges and his little friend Humpy, leading a merry life and liked by everybody for his good-tempered ways. And if the Tsar was a bit of a tartar, well, that didn't seem to matter – for a while. But, oh dear me, there came a day when it did matter; and it all happened through that firebird's feather, which, in spite of Humpy's warning, Jack had picked up and now always kept in his pocket.

Well, one morning, when Jack was having a friendly wrestling match with another young groom, the feather dropped out of his pocket, and lay in the sunshine of the courtyard, unnoticed by either of them. But that same evening the young groom happened to go into the courtyard – and what did he see? The whole place lit up and bright as noonday, and in the middle of the court a golden feather, blazing away more brilliantly than the brightest lamp.

Oh, oh, oh! The young groom picked up the feather and ran with it to the Tsar.

The Tsar said, 'Where did you find this?'

The groom said, 'In the courtyard; I think it must have fallen out of Jack's pocket.'

The Tsar sent for Jack. 'Jack, does this feather belong to you?'

'Yes, it does.'

'And where did you get it?'

'I found it in a field.'

'Well then, be off to the field and bring me the bird who dropped that feather.'

'Oh, your high and mightiness, I can't do that!'

'Can't? Do you say "can't" to *me*? Heads have rolled for speaking that word when your Tsar gives an order. Go, do as I bid you.'

Jack went off to tell Humpy. He was near to crying. 'Oh, Humpy dear, the Tsar has ordered me to bring him the firebird. And oh, Humpy dear, it seems that it's off with my head if I don't bring it.'

'Well, there you are, Jack, what did I tell you? You should never have picked up that feather. But come now, ask the Tsar for two troughs, a big jar full of honey, a pair of thick gloves, and a strong sack; also food for our journey. Then we'll be off.'

'Where to, Humpy dear?'

'Stupid! To catch a firebird.'

So Jack went to the Tsar and got the two troughs, and the jar of honey, and the pair of thick gloves, and the strong sack, and plenty of food for the journey. He brought all those things to Humpy; and whether Humpy made those things small, or whether on the other hand he made himself big, I can't tell you, because nobody has ever told me. But somehow or other, Humpy took everything on his back, and Jack along with them; and in less than no time he was whizzing away, sometimes through the air, and sometimes along the ground, for seven days and seven nights.

On the eighth day they came to a great forest, and in the forest was a wide glade, and beyond the glade rose a silver hill. At the foot of the hill flowed a sparkling stream; the grass in the glade shone brighter than any emerald: it fairly glittered. And as to the flowers that grew among the grass, they were of a beauty and a colour and a fragrance beyond all telling.

'Journey's end!' said Humpy, shaking everything, Jack included, off his back. 'For this is where the firebirds come at midnight to drink and bathe in the stream. So now, Jack, pour the honey into one trough, turn the other trough upside down and hide yourself under it. The birds will come to the honey trough, then you will creep out from under your trough, and with your gloved hands grab the bird nearest to you. It'll peck and claw and scream of course, but you mustn't mind that. Just give a shout and I'll come to help you. And so goodbye until midnight.'

Then Humpy galloped away up the silver mountain. And there was Jack all alone in the flowery glade.

Well, he set the troughs side by side on the bank of the stream, poured honey into one trough, turned the other trough upside down, crawled under it, put on the thick gloves and waited. . . .

The sun went down behind the silver hill; the flowers folded their petals; it was twilight; it was night; clouds hid the stars. Jack, crouched under his trough, felt cold and stiff; he peeped out – oh how dark it was, and how completely still!

No! Listen! Beyond the silver hill a screeching and a flurry of wings. And look! Behind the silver hill a great light that fanned out on every side, that grew and grew, that rose, that topped the hill, that poured down the hither side of the hill: the light of hundreds of flaming wings, as the firebirds, shrilly screaming, flew down into the valley, and running in a confusion of blazing lights and bobbing shadows, gathered round the honey trough, plunging their long beaks into the honey, and fighting and squabbling, without a thought but of getting the biggest share of the unexpected feast.

Slowly, cautiously, as if a monster snail was crawling there,

Jack, under his trough, moves nearer and nearer to the greedy, gulping, quarrelling birds. Now he is quite close to them; out darts his gloved hand, he grabs the long fiery tail of the bird nearest to him, the bird screams, tries to fly up, all the birds scream, all the birds except one fly up, over goes Jack's trough, over goes the honey trough, in a whirl of glittering feathers and piercing screams the flock of firebirds wheels round and up and away, all but the one bird which Jack still clutches by the tail; and though it pecks most viciously at his hand, its beak cannot pierce through the thick gloves. And, 'Humpy, Humpy!' shouts Jack in wild excitement, 'I have him, I've caught him, Humpy! Humpy! Humpy!'

And here's little Humpy galloping, sack in mouth. Into the sack then with the struggling protesting firebird, the neck of the sack firmly tied, and Jack and sack and firebird and all up on Humpy's back, and Humpy galloping away through the forest, and galloping, galloping over the ground – or is it through the air? Jack scarcely knows which, or where he is, they are going so swiftly; and here, in the dawn of that day, or the next, or the next after that – who can tell? – but here they are at last back in the courtyard of the Tsar's palace, and Jack is running into the palace and shouting, 'Tsar, Tsar! I've got him, I've got the firebird,' and dumping the sack down on a table, and the Tsar hurrying in his nightgown, followed by a crowd of startled courtiers, who, at Jack's command, close all the shutters, leaving the room in darkness.

Then, laughing and panting, Jack unties the sack, and on the instant there is such a fierce blaze of flaming light as sets everyone shouting 'Fire! Fire! Water! Water!'

But their fright turns to exclamations of wonder and delight as the firebird, somewhat bedraggled, struggles out of the sack and stands there on the table, defiantly preening its brilliant feathers.

II The Moon's Daughter

The Tsar had a gold collar and a gold chain made for the firebird.
It lit up the whole palace at night, and for a while the Tsar was
delighted with it. But it was forever pecking at him and scratching
him and screaming, so by and by the Tsar got tired of it, and set
it free to fly away to its silver mountain. So then he must have
something else to amuse him. What else? Why, a new wife to be
sure! And though the Tsar was old and fat and ugly, it went without saying that his new wife must be young and beautiful. So who
should she be? Who but the Moon's daughter, Alena the lovely.
And who should go and fetch that maiden for him? Who but Jack?

So the Tsar sent for Jack and said, 'Jack, I've a mind to marry
again. Go, fetch me the Moon's daughter.'

Jack said, 'Oh no! I don't think I can do that!'

The Tsar said, 'Oh yes! Do it you must, or I will have your
head!'

Jack, sad and sorrowful, went to Humpy in the stable.

Humpy said, 'What's the matter this time?'

Jack told him, and Humpy said, 'All this comes of picking up
that feather. I told you not to.'

Jack said, 'Dear Humpy, help me now, or the Tsar will have
my head.'

Humpy said, 'I don't know that you deserve help; but I *will*
help you. Now listen to me. Princess Alena the lovely, daughter
of the Moon, lives sometimes in the sea and sometimes in the sky.
And sometimes when the days are still and the sea is calm, she rows
over the sea in a golden boat with silver oars. Then she will bring
her boat into the shallows and step on shore to rest and refresh
herself and play sweet music on her dulcimer. It is then that we
may catch her. Go, ask the Tsar for a gold-embroidered tent, a
dainty little table, an ivory chair, curiously wrought, a padded
footstool, some sweetmeats and rare wine; also a few silver dishes
and a goblet or two of precious glass. And hurry, for it is time we
set off.'

So Jack got all these things from the Tsar, and Humpy took them on his back, and Jack as well, and off they went, galloping, galloping, and after a long time, or a short time, came to the shore of the great ocean. And the day was bright and the sea calm.

So there on the shore, where the short green grass met the white sand, Jack, on Humpy's orders, pitched the gold-embroidered tent, and set within it the ivory chair, curiously wrought, and the padded footstool, and the dainty little table spread with the silver dishes filled with sweetmeats, and the goblets of precious glass, and the rare wine.

And when all this was done, Humpy said, 'Look over the ocean. Do you see a glittering of gold and a twinkling of silver?'

Jack said, 'Yes, I see.'

Humpy said, 'That is the princess's little boat making this way. So now, Jack, behind the tent with you, crouch down; let the princess come into the tent, let her refresh herself with the wine and the sweetmeats, let her play her dulcimer and sing her songs; and when she is rapt away by the sound of her own sweet singing, run into the tent, take her in your arms, and call for me. Be heedful, be swift. If you lose this chance you may not get another.'

Then Humpy galloped away, and Jack went to crouch behind the gold-embroidered tent.

Now on the blue sea the glitter of the golden boat and the twinkling of the silver oars drew nearer and nearer. Now the beautiful princess Alena brought her boat to land, and lifting up her flowing robes with one hand, and taking her dulcimer in the other, stepped ashore. Wondering, she sees the gold-embroidered tent, steps up to it, peeps inside. 'Oh,' thinks she, 'my dear mother Moon must have put this here to surprise and delight me!'

And in she goes, and down she sits, tastes the sweetmeats, sips the wine; and, refreshed and happy, takes up her dulcimer and plays and sings.

Ah, how deftly she plays, how sweetly she sings! Her thoughts are carried far away on the wings of her own sweet singing. Now, Jack, this is your chance!

But – did you ever? – Jack, too, has been carried away by that sweet singing: lulled into a vague and dreamy happiness, he has actually fallen asleep! And sleep he does till sunset; and then it is Humpy's indignant prodding hoof that wakes him.

'Fool! The sun has gone down, the evening star is shining, the princess has gathered up her flowing robes and stepped back into her golden boat; the boat is now but a speck on the horizon. . . . Well, after all, you can go your own way, it is not *I* who will lose my head!'

Poor Jack bursts out a-blubbering. Oh me, will Humpy forgive him, for surely he will never forgive himself; and now, what's to be done?

'Wait till tomorrow,' says Humpy, 'when maybe the princess will come once more. But if you fall asleep again, I'll leave you lying and go home without you.'

Then Humpy kicked up his heels and galloped off. Jack spent a miserable night. But in the morning, as he paced the shore and looked out over the quiet ocean – what does he see? A glittering of gold and a twinkling of silver. Yes, it is the princess Alena's little boat coming this way.

Jack runs behind the tent. He snatches up sharp stones and bits of board from old wrecks; the boards have nails sticking up in them – so much the better! Jack piles up stones and boards into an uneasy, lumpy, nail-bristling couch, and sprawls face downward on it. 'Now,' thinks he, 'fall asleep if you can!'

Alena, that lovely princess, brings her boat to land, she gathers up her flowing robes, she steps ashore, she trips lightly to the tent, she takes her seat, eats, drinks, picks up her dulcimer, and softly, sweetly, begins to play and sing.

Ah, how drowsy that gentle playing, that sweet, low singing makes our Jack! His eyes close, his head nods . . . is he going to fall asleep again? Not he! The jagged stones and the rusty nails prod his drowsy body with sharp reminders: '*Keep awake! Keep awake!*' He leaps to his feet, he rushes into the tent, he flings his arms about the beautiful Alena, he bawls at the top of his voice, 'Humpy! Humpy!'

And here comes Humpy galloping. Jack is up on Humpy's

back, the lovely Alena is clasped in his arms, Humpy is up in the
air and away. As for the gold-embroidered tent, and all that it
contains, it can wait for the storms of autumn to carry it out to
sea, and the fishes can feast on what's left of the sweetmeats. . . .

Now in the royal palace the beautiful princess Alena, the Moon's
daughter, sits at table with the Tsar. She is sulking – and no
wonder! The stupid old Tsar has been making one would-be pretty
speech after another, but she doesn't seem to be listening. The Tsar
speaks of their marriage, of the guests who are already invited, of
the feast that is already being prepared. The princess Alena, the
Moon's daughter, opens her proud lips.

'My jewels, my head ornaments, my robes of state, my golden
slippers – all things fitting for my bridal – are in a chest at the
bottom of the sea. Let them be fetched.'

Well then, the Tsar says, if it will please her, of course they shall
be fetched, and Jack must fetch them.

Oh, this is too much! Jack almost says 'No.' And it isn't the
Tsar's shouting and bawling at him that makes him change his
mind and agree to go; it is something in the look of the princess
as she turns her beautiful eyes upon him. 'Go for my sake, Jack,'
that look seems to be saying. 'Do just this one thing for me, dear
Jack, that misery may be turned into joy.'

So Jack bows to the Tsar (yes, Jack is learning courtly manners)
and says 'I will set out at once.'

And then the lovely Alena speaks again. 'On your way, perhaps
you will kindly pay a visit to my mother, the Moon, and ask her
why for three long nights she hasn't let her face be seen, but keeps
it hidden behind dusky clouds.'

'I will ask her, my princess,' says Jack, and bows once more,
and goes out to little Humpy in the stables.

'So we must be off again, Jack,' says Humpy.

'Seems we must,' says Jack.

'I think this will be the last time,' says Humpy.

'Well, I hope so with all my heart,' says Jack.

'Then up you get, Jack, and we'll be off.'

So off they went, galloping, galloping – whether for a short time or a long time, who knows? – and came at last to the verge of a great stretch of sea with more land on the farther side of it. And there they saw a wonder; for across the sea, making a bridge from one land to the other land, lay a monstrous whale. On his tail there grew a forest. On his back was built a town. On his brow youths and maidens were dancing. And in the darkness of his mouth children were gathering mushrooms. So over the whale bridge Jack and Humpy trotted from one land to the other land; and when they reached the farther shore the whale asked, in a hoarse and melancholy voice, 'Whither bound?'

And Humpy answered, 'To the farthest east, to the silver palace of the Lady Moon.'

And the whale spoke again in his hoarse and melancholy voice, 'Ask her then from me how long I must lie here helpless to be trampled on by these unfeeling feet. Ask her what sin I have committed, and how I may atone.'

And Humpy answered, 'Yes, we will ask her,' and gave a leap.

And now he was speeding up towards the sky, higher and higher, with Jack clinging to his long ears, and bursting into song for the delight of buffeting into and through the woolly white clouds, and galloping over the blue meadows that stretched above the clouds on every side of them.

Now see – in the distance a silver gleaming; and every moment coming nearer and nearer the high shining towers of the palace of the Lady Moon. And now they have reached the palace, and there on her palace balcony sits Lady Moon, telling fortunes with a pack of cards, her round good-tempered face all dimpled with amiable smiles.

So Humpy comes to a stop under the balcony, and Jack alights, hat in hand, and making his best bow.

'Welcome, Jack the farmer's son, for so I take you to be,' says Lady Moon. 'Come up to stand by me, and tell me what brings you here.'

So Jack goes up on to the balcony, and tells the Lady Moon that he comes with a message from her daughter, the princess Alena.

The princess would know why for three days and three nights Lady Moon hasn't let her face be seen, but keeps it hidden behind dusky clouds.

'Ah, Jack, my dear,' says Lady Moon, 'I have been sore troubled over the fate of my dearest Alena; and that is why I have hidden my face. For I could not well bear to think that my beautiful daughter should be married in her seventeenth year to that old, selfish, ugly-tempered Tsar, who is seventy if he is a day. But now the cards tell me otherwise, and so I can smile again. Carry back to my daughter her mother's love, Jack – and if you give her your own love at the same time, so much the better.'

Then Jack asked about the whale, and Lady Moon said, 'The whale is punished because he has swallowed, and keeps prisoner in his belly, a fleet of thirty ships belonging to Lord Sun. Let him give up those ships and he shall be pardoned. . . . But now away with you, Jack, for your tasks are still unfinished. Tell my dearest daughter not to grieve; tell her she shall not marry any old baboon of a Tsar; tell her that her mother promises her a young and hand-some husband. But I'm not telling you, Jack, who that young and handsome husband shall be.'

With that, Lady Moon's round face was all lit up with smiles. And she kissed Jack on both cheeks and bade him be off with him.

So Humpy and Jack sped back across the blue sky meadows, and down through the woolly white clouds, and so to earth, and came to where the great whale bridged the sea between the two lands. The whale was looking very miserable, but he cheered up when he saw Jack and Humpy. And when he heard about the ships he gave a tremendous laugh, and a tremendous hiccup; and out of his great mouth came gliding thirty golden ships – the fleet belonging to the Lord Sun. And the ships hoisted their golden sails, and moved away across the water, with the sailors tossing up their caps and shouting, '*Hurrah!*'

'Ha! Ha! Ha! Ha!' laughed the whale, and was going to plunge down into the sea; but Humpy cried out, 'Stop! Stop! Do you want to drown a town full of people, and a company of dancing youths and maidens, and all those little mushroom gatherers? Is that your gratitude?'

'Oh dear!' said the whale. 'I'd forgotten all about them!'

Then Humpy galloped from end to end of the whale's great body, and ordered all the people in the town, and all the dancing youths and maidens, and all the children who were picking mushrooms to get back on land; and they went, a great procession of them. And Humpy said to the whale, 'Now, old fellow, you're free, and you can just show your gratitude to Jack and me by going down to the bottom of the ocean and bringing up a casket belonging to the Moon's daughter, Alena the beautiful.'

So the whale plunged down, and in less than no time came up again with a golden casket in his mouth. And Humpy said, 'Take the casket, Jack, and we'll be off.'

But Jack cried out, 'No, I won't take it! I don't want to take it!'

'Well, and why not?' said Humpy.

'Because,' said Jack, and he was almost crying, 'because – the wedding guests are already invited, the wedding feast is already prepared, and in her jewels, her head ornaments, her robes of state, and her golden slippers, the princess Alena is to marry the fat old Tsar – and oh, my heart is breaking!'

Humpy laughed. 'The Lady Moon promised something different,' he said. 'The Lady Moon promised her daughter a young and handsome husband.'

'I don't care how handsome or how young he is,' mumbled Jack. 'I hate him whoever he is! I hate him!'

But he took the casket, and they said goodbye to the happy whale and Humpy galloped off, sometimes whizzing through the air, and sometimes whizzing over the earth, till there they were, back in the Tsar's city.

Every bell in the city was ringing; in the streets fountains of wine gushed ruby red; round the fountains the people were dancing; in the palace the feast was spread; in the church the priest was waiting; the palace gates were open wide; the princess Alena has received her casket, and see now, out through the palace gates issues the grand procession: the ugly old Tsar riding in a golden carriage, the lovely princess, wearing her glittering jewels, her head ornaments, her robes of state, her golden slippers, is seated beside him; and behind them come coachload after coachload of lords and ladies, and neighbouring princes, and court officials, with soldiers in rank upon rank marching before and behind and on every side. Humpy is dancing with excitement, but Jack turns away his head; no he won't look, there are tears in his eyes.

The grand procession reaches the church door, the Tsar is handing the princess out of the carriage, it seems that her fate is sealed. . . . But – see there, see there! – floating down from the clear sky, and coming nearer and nearer, is a great silver light, and in the silver light a winged chariot, and seated in the chariot the Lady Moon. The Lady Moon leans from the chariot, she stretches out her arms, she snatches up the ugly old Tsar and

33

carries him away, away, away, right up to her palace in the sky. And there she gives him a shake and sets him down, and puts him to mind her flock of geese forever more.

Must the priest then close his book and go home? Must the wedding guests depart, and the wedding feast remain untasted? Not a bit of it! The princess has chosen for herself, she knows whom she loves, she knows whom she will marry. She goes to where Jack stands weeping, she puts her hand in his, she leads him into the church, she says to the priest, 'Here is my beloved, here is the one who is to be my husband. Come now, do your duty, marry us, marry us!'

And Jack with all his tears turned to smiles, answers 'Yes, oh yes, marry us, marry us!'

Then all the people cheered, and the wedding guests laughed and clapped their hands, and the bells rang out merrily, merrily, and Jack and Alena the beautiful were married, and the wedding feast was not wasted, and everyone made merry.

And Jack and his lovely princess and little Humpy lived happily, none more happily, ever after.

3 · Mainu the Frog

It was Kiman, the son of Kimanze, and he would take a wife.
Would he take an earthly maiden? No, he would not. He would
take the daughter of Lord Sun and Lady Moon, because once,
when she was looking down out of heaven, Kiman had seen her
face looking up at him out of a pool, and she was very lovely,
white and golden, with the blue of the sky all round her. And
since that day he could think of no one else.

So he called Eagle to him and said, 'You, far-flier, will you
carry a message to Lord Sun?'

Eagle said, 'No, I will not.'

Then Kiman called Antelope to him, and said, 'You, swift-
runner, will you carry a message to Lord Sun?'

Antelope said, 'No, I will not.'

Then Kiman asked animal after animal, and bird after bird. But
none of them would carry his message.

Now he was in despair. He went to sit on the bank of a pond.
He said, 'Since no one will carry my message, I may as well drown
myself.'

Then Mainu the Frog scrambled out of the water and said,
'You haven't asked *me* to carry your message.'

Kiman said, 'You! How can *you* get to heaven, when people
who have wings cannot?'

Frog said, 'I know the way, they do not. Write your message
and bring it to me.'

So Kiman went home and wrote a letter saying, 'I, Kiman, son
of Kimanze on earth, I wish to marry the daughter of Lord Sun
and Lady Moon.' He brought the letter to the pond where Frog
was waiting. Frog put the letter in his mouth and hopped away.

35

He hopped, hopped, hopped for a long time. He reached the well where the people of Lord Sun and Lady Moon come down from heaven to fetch water.

And he got into the well and kept quiet.

By and by the girls, the water-carriers, came down from heaven. They came down by a cobweb that Spider had woven. They were carrying empty water jugs. They put the jugs in the well, and Frog got into one of them. The girls filled their jugs; they didn't know that Frog was in one of them. They lifted the full jugs out of the well, and carried them back up the cobweb to heaven. Frog went with them, hidden in the jug.

In a room in the palace of Lord Sun and Lady Moon, the girls, the water-carriers, put down the jugs on the floor and went away. Frog was swimming round in his jug; now he came out of it. There was a table in the room. Frog jumped on to the table and spat the letter out of his mouth. He left the letter lying on the table, and went to hide in a corner of the room.

By and by in came Lord Sun. He drank some water. He looked on the table, saw the letter. He called the girls, 'This letter – who brought it?'

'Master, we don't know.' The girls went away.

Lord Sun opens the letter. He reads: 'I, Kiman, son of Kimanze on earth, I wish to marry the daughter of Lord Sun and Lady Moon.'

Lord Sun thinks, 'Kiman, son of Kimanze, is a man that lives on earth. I am a man that lives in heaven. How did this letter come here?' He went away to show the letter to Lady Moon.

Frog stayed in his corner. He stayed many hours. The sky people came and went, taking water from the jugs. And when all the jugs were empty, Frog took a hop and got into one of them.

By and by the girls, the water-carriers, came to fetch the jugs. They went down to earth on the cobweb that Spider had woven. They came to the well, and put the jugs in the water. Frog got out. He stayed at the bottom of the well until the girls had re-filled the jugs and gone back up the cobweb to heaven. Then he went to call on Kiman.

'Kiman, son of Kimanze, I delivered your letter and Lord Sun read it. But he has not yet sent an answer.'

Kiman said, 'How do I know that you are not telling lies?'

Frog said, 'Wait and see.'

Kiman waited six days: it seemed like six years. He was stamping with impatience. He wrote another letter: 'Lord Sun and Lady Moon, I, Kiman, son of Kimanze, wrote to you, but you did not answer. You did not say, "We accept you"; you did not say, "We refuse you." Say one or the other, that I may know whether I am to live or die.'

Kiman gave the letter to Frog. Frog took it in his mouth and went to hide in the well. The girls, the water-carriers, came down from heaven with their jugs. They put the jugs in the water. Frog got into a jug. The girls filled the jugs; they didn't see that Frog was in one of them. They lifted the full jugs out of the well, and went back up the cobweb to heaven.

In a room in the palace of Lord Sun and Lady Moon, the girls, the water-carriers, put down the jugs on the floor and went away. Frog came out of the jug. He jumped on to the table and spat the letter out of his mouth. He left the letter lying on the table, and went to hide in a corner.

By and by in comes Lord Sun. 'What, another letter!' He picks it up, reads. He calls the water-carriers. 'You girls, since when have you taken to carrying letters about?'

'Master, we have never carried letters.'

Lord Sun is troubled. He writes a letter: 'Kiman, son of Kimanze, you who send me letters about marrying my daughter. How can I agree before I know you? Come yourself, bringing with you the first-present. When I know you, I can say ,"Yes".'

Lord Sun lays his letter on the table. He goes away. Frog comes out of the corner where he is hiding, climbs up on to the table, takes the letter in his mouth and creeps into an empty water jug. People come and go, taking water from the jugs. When all the jugs are empty, the girls, the water-carriers, come in to fetch them. They go with the jugs down to earth by the cobweb Spider has woven.

The girls come to the well, they put the jugs in the water. Frog gets out of his jug and goes to the bottom of the well. The girls, the water-carriers, fill all the jugs and go back up the cobweb to heaven. Frog comes out of the well. It is now night. Frog goes to Kiman's house and knocks on the door: *Flim, flam! Flim, flam!*

Kiman is in bed. He calls, 'Who knocks?'

Frog says, 'Mainu, the Frog.'

Kiman opens the door. Frog gives him the letter. Kiman reads, leaps for joy. He says, 'Frog, take what you will from my larder. Sleep anywhere in my house that pleases you. I will go back to my bed. Tomorrow we will decide upon the first-present.'

Frog went to Kiman's larder: he didn't like what he found there. But he drank some milk, and he slept where it was cool and pleasant in the draught from the door. In the morning Kiman put forty pearls into a bag. He also wrote a letter.

This is what he wrote: 'To you, Lord Sun and Lady Moon, I, Kiman, son of Kimanze, send the first-present. But I myself do not bring it, because I must stay at home to get together the wooing-present. You then send to tell me the amount of the wooing-present, and you shall have it.'

Kiman laid the letter on top of the bag that held the pearls and said, 'Frog, carry this bag to Lord Sun as a first-present.'

Frog said, 'My mouth is scarcely big enough to carry it.'

Kiman said, 'You must carry it.'

So Frog opened his mouth wide, wide, and stuffed the bag into it. Now he couldn't speak, he could only grunt. He went to the well and hid. The girls, the water-carriers, came down from heaven by the cobweb. They put the jugs in the water. Frog got into a jug, his jaws were aching; he took the bag out of his mouth and tucked it under his arm.

The girls fill the jugs; they go back up to heaven. In a room in the palace of Lord Sun and Lady Moon they put down the jugs on the floor, and go away. Frog comes out of the jug, jumps on to the table, lays down the bag of pearls and the letter, and goes to hide in a corner of the room.

By and by in come Lord Sun and Lady Moon, walking arm in

arm. They drink water. Lord Sun looks on the table. He says,
'Again a letter!' He reads the letter, opens the bag, sees the pearls.
He says, 'Who is it comes with these things? I have never seen him.
I don't know his name or what he is like. But he has come a long
way; he must be hungry and should be fed.'

Lady Moon said, 'I will cook a chicken and some sweetcorn and
leave it here on the table.'

Lord Sun said, 'Yes, you do that.'

They went away. Very soon Lord Sun came back with a letter
he had written. The letter said, 'Thou, son-in-law, the first-present
which thou hast sent me I have received. The amount of the
wooing-present which thou shalt give me is a sack of gold.'

Lord Sun put the letter on the table and went away.

The time passed. The sky people came and went, fetching water
from the jugs until all the jugs were empty. Then in came Lady
Moon carrying two dishes: in the one, fried chicken; in the other,
sweetcorn. She set the dishes on the table and went away. Frog
came out of his corner, jumped on the table. He ate the sweetcorn
and left the chicken. He took the letter Lord Sun had written, came
down from the table, and jumped into an empty jug. Now he was
tired, he fell asleep. He was still sleeping when the girls, the water-
carriers, came to fetch the empty jugs. He was still sleeping when
they carried the jugs down to earth by the cobweb Spider had
woven. He only woke when the girls put the jugs into the well.
Then he got out of his jug and hid. The girls filled their jugs and
carried them back up the cobweb to heaven. Frog came out of the
well and went to Kiman's house.

He knocked: *Flim, flam! Flim, flam!*

'Who knocks?'

'Mainu the Frog.'

'Come in.'

Frog went in. He gave Kiman Lord Sun's letter. Kiman read.
He rejoiced. He said, 'It will take me six days to collect a sack of
gold.'

Frog said, 'And when you have collected it, who is to carry it
to heaven?'

Kiman said, 'You.'

Frog said, 'I cannot carry it. I am not big enough.'

Kiman raved and said, 'Frog, Frog, will you fail me now? I will not live another day!'

Frog said, 'Calm yourself, collect the money. I, Mainu the Frog, am not easily beaten. Give me a piece of gold, and I will find a way of getting the sack to heaven.'

Kiman gave Frog a piece of gold, and Frog went away. He went to call on Omari, the medicine man. It took him three days to get to Omari's house. When he got there, he gave Omari the piece of gold, and in return Omari taught Frog two spells: one to make big things small, the other to make small things big. He also taught Frog two ways of breathing: one to make blind, the other to make see again.

Then Frog went back to Kiman and said, 'Is the wooing-present, the sack of gold, ready?'

Kiman said, 'Yes, it is.'

Frog said, 'Bring it here.'

Kiman brought it. It was forty times as big as Frog. But Frog put his hands on it and said the first spell that Omari had taught him, the spell to make things small. And the sack shrunk till it was no bigger than Frog's thumb.

Kiman was frightened. He cried out, 'Oh, oh, all my gold is shrunk away! Now I have nothing to offer to Lord Sun!'

But Frog said, 'Stupid! You have plenty to offer. I will show you how much.' He said the second spell Omari had taught him, and the sack swelled out to its proper size. Then he said the first spell again, and the sack shrunk. Frog put the sack in his mouth and was hopping away, when Kiman said, 'Stop! Stop! You may indeed carry the wooing-present, but who will bring back the bride?'

Frog said, 'Have I failed you yet?'

Kiman said 'No.'

Frog said, 'Neither will I fail you now.'

And he went away.

He went to the well. The girls, the water-carriers, came. They filled their jugs, they went back up the cobweb to heaven. They did not know that Frog was in one of the jugs.

The girls set down the jugs in the room of the water. Frog gets out of his jug; he hides in a corner. He waits until Lord Sun and Lady Moon have gone to bed.

Now it is night. All sleep except Frog. Frog comes out of the room of the water. He searches here, searches there; he comes to the room where the daughter of Lord Sun and Lady Moon is sleeping. He hops on to her pillow. He breathes on her eyes. He breathes the first way Omari the medicine man had taught him, the way to make blind. Then he goes back to the room of the water, hides in his corner, and sleeps.

Now comes morning. All the people get up. But the daughter of Lord Sun and Lady Moon does not get up. They say, 'What, do you not get up?'

She says, 'My eyes are closed, I cannot see.' They call Lord Sun and Lady Moon. They come. They say, 'What is this? Daughter, open your eyes!' She says, 'I cannot! I cannot! I cannot!'

Lord Sun called two messengers. He said, 'Take offerings of meat and jewels and go to my wizard, where he sits on his cloud. Ask him the meaning of our daughter's sickness. Ask him also the cure.'

The messengers take the offerings of meat and jewels. They set off, they come to where Lord Sun's wizard sits on his cloud. They bow low, they present the offerings, and the wizard says, 'What do you wish of me?'

The messengers answer, 'The eyes of the daughter of Lord Sun and Lady Moon are shut and will not open. Therefore she cannot see. We would know how to open her eyes that she may see again.'

The wizard said, 'The maiden is promised in marriage, but not married. The longing of him to whom she is promised has caused this mischief. Let her be given to him, and her eyes will open. . . . I have spoken.'

The messengers went back to Lord Sun and told the words of the wizard. Lord Sun said, 'Very well. But now it is evening. We will all sleep. Tomorrow we will send our daughter down to earth.'

Frog had crept close. He heard everything that was said. He

went unseen into an empty jug; he was very tired, he slept soundly.

In the morning early, Lord Sun said to Spider, 'Weave a very large cobweb to reach to earth; for today is the taking down of my daughter to her bridegroom.'

So Spider began to weave a new large web. It took him all day. In the meantime, the girls, the water-carriers, took the empty jugs and went down to earth by the old web. and Frog went with them in one of the jugs. The girls came to the well, they put the jugs in the water. Frog came out of the jug in which he was hidden. He stayed at the bottom of the well until the girls had filled all the jugs and gone back up the cobweb to heaven. Then he came up out of the water and went to Kiman's house.

He knocked. *Flim, flam! Flim, flam!* 'Kiman, son of Kimanze, open your door. Your bride, the white and gold maiden, daughter of Lord Sun and Lady Moon, today she comes.'

'Frog, I fear you are lying. And if you are lying I will have your life!'

'Master, I am truth itself. As for your bride, this evening I will bring her.'

Frog went back to the well. He hid. He waited all day. When the sun set Spider finished weaving his new large web. The people of Lord Sun and Lady Moon gathered – a multitude. They came down to earth by the new large web, bringing with them the daughter of Lord Sun and Lady Moon, whose eyes were still closed.

They bore her to the well, they put her down, they left her, and went back up the cobweb. She sits and weeps, seeing nothing. But Frog comes out of the well. He says, 'I am Mainu the Frog; I am your guide to him who loves you.' He blows, as Omari the medicine man had taught him, the breath that makes the blind see. The maiden's eyes open, she looks round her, she laughs for joy.

Frog said, 'Come.' And she rose and followed him. He brought her to Kiman's house. They embraced, they married, they were very happy.

And Frog said, 'Now there is the joy of one, and the joy of two: the joy of the bride, the joy of the bridegroom. And who brought all this joy to pass? I, Mainu the Frog.'

43

4 · *Lilla Rosa*

A king and a queen had one little daughter, who was called Lilla Rosa; and if you had searched the world over, you couldn't have found a more beautiful child than that child. And beside being beautiful she was kind and good, so that everyone loved her.

They were very happy, those three, the king, the queen, and their lovely little daughter. But there came a time of sorrow, for the queen died, and the king, who should have known better (but didn't know better), took another wife, a very wicked woman, a widow with a daughter called Long Leda, who was as ugly and bad as Lilla Rosa was beautiful and good. The two princesses grew up together in the royal palace. But ah, how the new queen, the wicked stepmother, and her ugly daughter, Long Leda, hated poor Lilla Rosa!

They bullied her and made a regular slave of her, ordering her to fetch and carry for them, and do all sorts of heavy tasks that a young princess ought not to do. But Lilla Rosa never complained; she did her best to love and please them, and that made the stepmother hate her all the more bitterly.

Now one day the stepmother queen and the two girls were walking in the garden, and they heard the head gardener speaking to his man, telling him to fetch an axe that had been left in the wood. But the queen said 'Your man is busy about other things. Lilla Rosa shall fetch the axe.'

The gardener said, 'That is scarcely an errand befitting the daughter of a king, your majesty!'

The queen said, 'Mind your own business! When I give an order I expect to be obeyed. Go at once, Lilla Rosa, and bring the axe here.'

So Lilla Rosa went to the wood, and found the axe lying under an oak tree. And there were three white doves perching on the handle of it.

'Dear little birds,' said Lilla Rosa, 'you must fly away, because I have to take this axe to my stepmother. But before you go, here is something for you.' And she took a piece of cake from her pocket, crumbled it, and held it out on the palm of her hand to the doves.

The doves flew up from the handle of the axe. They hovered over Lilla Rosa's outstretched hand and ate up the crumbs. Then they said, 'Coo-roo, coo-roo,' fluttered their wings, and flew up into the oak tree. And Lilla Rosa walked away with the axe.

In the tree the doves were talking.

'Coo-roo, coo-roo! What reward shall we give this kind and lovely maiden?'

And the first dove said, 'I will give that she shall be even more beautiful than she is now: so beautiful that the world has never seen her like.'

And the second dove said, 'I will give that her hair shall be fine-spun gold.'

And the third dove said, 'I will give that when she laughs pearls and diamonds shall fall from her lips.'

Then the doves fluttered their wings and flew away.

So when Lilla Rosa came back with the axe, everyone who saw her was amazed. She was the same Lilla Rosa, and yet she was something more. She shone in beauty like the sun itself, her hair gleamed golden, and when she gave a little laugh – what fell from her lips? Pearls and diamonds! The stepmother was enraged. If she had hated Lilla Rosa before, she hated her now with a three-fold hatred. And as to Long Leda – she looked by comparison simply hideous. The stepmother couldn't bear it. She gave Lilla Rosa a hard smack, and told her to go indoors and wash her hair. Lilla Rosa did go and wash her hair – and it shone more brilliantly than ever.

So then the stepmother called the head gardener and told him to take the axe back into the wood, and leave it where he had left it before. And she told him also what he must say when she and Long Leda came once more to walk in the garden.

'And mind you,' said she, 'if you don't do and say exactly as I bid you, I will have you whipped with seven rods.'

Well, the head gardener wasn't very willing – but what could the poor man do? A queen was a queen and must be obeyed. So he took the axe and laid it under the oak tree.

Next day the stepmother and Long Leda went again to walk in the garden, and the head gardener and his man were planting rose bushes. So when the head gardener saw them coming, he said very loudly, 'Bob, I left my axe under the oak tree in the wood, go and fetch it.'

And the stepmother said, 'No, no, your man is busy. The princess Long Leda shall fetch the axe.'

And the head gardener said (as he had been told to say), 'That is scarcely an errand befitting the daughter of a king, your majesty!'

But the stepmother said, 'Mind your own business! When I give an order I expect to be obeyed. Go at once, Long Leda, and bring the axe here.'

So off went Long Leda, grumbling and muttering to herself.

Well, she came to where the axe lay under the oak tree; and there were the three white doves perching on the handle of it.

'Be off with you!' shouted Long Leda, and she took up a handful of earth and threw it at the doves. The doves flew up into the tree, and Long Leda walked off with the axe.

In the tree the doves were talking.

'*Coo-roo, coo-roo!* What punishment shall we give to that rude maiden?'

And the first dove said, 'I will give that she shall be twice as ugly as she was before.'

And the second dove said, 'I will give that her hair shall be like a thorn bush.'

And the third dove said, 'I will give that every time she laughs a toad shall jump out of her mouth.'

Then the doves fluttered their wings and flew away.

When Long Leda went back into the garden, the head gardener and his man gave one look at her and rushed away; and as to the queen, she gave a shriek and fainted. For the ugliness of Long

Leda's face was something that cannot be described, and her hair stuck out all round her head like a thorn bush; and when she laughed to see the gardeners running, a great toad sprang out of her mouth. So like enough it is true what we are told – that she never laughed again.

Well, well, if the stepmother queen had hated Lilla Rosa before, she hated her from that day with a more deadly hatred. She said to herself 'Lilla Rosa must die, and Lilla Rosa *shall* die!' And she called a shipmaster to her. The shipmaster was getting ready to sail into a far distant land, and the stepmother said to him, 'I will give you a thousand gold pieces if you will take the princess Lilla Rosa with you and throw her overboard in mid-ocean. But if you refuse to do it, I will have you broken on the wheel.'

The shipmaster said, 'Give me the thousand gold pieces then; for I have no wish to be broken on the wheel.' And that very night, when Lilla Rosa was sleeping soundly (for the queen had given her a sleeping draught) he carried her to his ship and set sail. But she looked so lovely, so lovely, as she lay there sleeping, that he said to himself, 'No, I cannot do it. I will carry her to the distant land and leave her there. When I come home without her – how is the queen to know that she still lives?'

Yes, that's what the shipmaster planned to do; but his plans miscarried. For when the ship was in mid-ocean, a most terrible storm arose, the ship was wrecked, and the captain and his crew scrambled into the longboat and rowed off, giving no thought to Lilla Rosa.

Was that the end then of poor Lilla Rosa? No, it wasn't. It seemed that even the rough and roaring waves had pity on her. They floated her away and away, and tossed her up at last on the sandy shore of a little green island.

On that green island Lilla Rosa lived all alone, eating wild berries and roots, drinking the water of a bright little spring, and sleeping among the ferns. But sometimes she felt very sad; and often she stood on the sandy beach looking out over the sparkling waves, hoping to see some ship sailing her way. And no ship came.

But something came: one day, as she so stood on the edge of

the tide, the waves, tossing and complaining, threw up two objects at her feet. One was a coconut; the other a slender little figurehead from some wrecked vessel. The figurehead was that of a mermaid. The mermaid was wearing a golden crown; she had her hands crossed over her breast, and though her blue eyes looked rather stern, her lips were smiling.

And both the coconut and the figurehead Lilla Rosa picked up and carried to a ferny dell where she used to sleep. With a sharp splinter of stone she pierced the holes in the top of the coconut and drank the milk. That was good! Then she took a big stone and hammered and hammered until she had broken open the coconut. She ate a little of it, and then she thought, 'Surely I should share this treat with the birds!' So what did she do? She took the mermaid, set her up on her tail, and tied her with her girdle to the stump of a tree. She put the broken-up coconut on the mermaid's crown, and said, 'Now little birds, here's your breakfast!' Then she went off a little way, and sat down among the ferns to watch.

The sun was warm, the air was balmy, and the waves breaking on the shore said, '*Hush!*' and again '*Hush!*' Lilla Rosa yawned, shut her eyes and fell asleep.

She dreamed that she was listening to a very sweet song, more beautiful than she had ever yet heard. She woke, and still she heard the singing. She got up, and led by the sound, went back to where she had left the mermaid on the tree stump. What did she see? No tree stump, no mermaid, no coconut, but a blossoming, sweet-smelling linden tree; and perched on the topmost branch of that tree sat a nightingale, singing, singing. But it was not only the nightingale that sang: every small leaf of the tree was making music – in fact it was the most glorious harmony of sound that anyone ever heard this side of heaven.

'Oh!' said Lilla Rosa. 'Oh! I don't think I shall ever feel sad again!'

And every day after that, if she should ever begin to feel sad and lonely, she had only to go and sit under the linden tree, and listen to the singing nightingale and the music-making leaves, and all her sadness was changed to joy.

In those days she didn't stand on the edge of the sea quite so often, looking for the ship that didn't come; so that when at last a ship did come, she didn't see it, because she was sitting under the linden tree, listening to the song of the nightingale and the music of the leaves.

It was a magnificent white ship that came sailing, a ship owned by a young prince. And the prince himself was on board, sailing for his pleasure here and there about the world. The sea was calm and the wind off shore, and as the ship drew near the island the marvellous singing flowed out over the water. And the captain said, 'Your highness, this must be an enchanted land!' And he would have turned the ship and sailed away, but the prince said, 'No, no, I must go on shore and find out where this music comes from.'

And go on shore he did, and came to where the nightingale and the linden leaves were singing. And there was Lilla Rosa sitting under the linden tree.

'O-oh!' The prince's heart seemed to leap right out of his body, for never had he thought that anyone could be so beautiful. And as to Lilla Rosa, she was so overjoyed to see a human being after her months of loneliness, that she jumped to her feet and ran to the prince with both hands outstretched. She told the prince her sad story, and he said, 'I will take you home; you shall never be lonely again.' And he brought her to his ship and set sail for his own country.

You may be sure Lilla Rosa was glad to go; and yet, and yet. . . . Well, it saddened her a little to think that never again would she hear that wonderful music.

What? Never again? Dear Lilla Rosa, that needn't trouble you! The music is flowing out over the water; and behold, wonder of wonders, the linden tree has uprooted itself, and here it comes flying through the air after the ship, with the nightingale still perched on its topmost branch, and the bird and the leaves are singing their loudest and sweetest.

So to the sound of that music the prince brought Lilla Rosa home to his palace; and the tree drifted down into the palace garden, and there the prince and Lilla Rosa took spades and planted it.

To the sound of that music they fell in love and married; and by and by Lilla Rosa gave birth to a beautiful baby boy.

Now the cup of their happiness seemed full to overflowing. And in her happiness Lilla Rosa wrote a letter to the king, her father, telling him of everything that had happened to her, but never telling that the stepmother queen was the cause of all her troubles. For she thought, 'Why should I make more mischief? We must let bygones be bygones.'

When the king read the letter he rejoiced. He wanted to take ship at once and visit Lilla Rosa. But the stepmother said, 'What! And let your kingdom go to wrack and ruin in your absence? No, no, that won't do! Long Leda and I will go; and we will bring Lilla Rosa and her husband and the child back to visit *you*.'

And though the king was unwilling he had to agree; for, to tell truth, he was afraid of his wife.

So the stepmother and Long Leda prepared to set out. But first the stepmother went to consult a witch who was a special friend of hers. And from the witch she got a robe of many-coloured silk, embroidered with gold. The robe was beautiful to look at – but woe to the one who put that garment on!

The stepmother showed the robe to the king, and said, 'I am taking this as a present from us both to Lilla Rosa.'

The king said 'Very pretty! But mind you bring Lilla Rosa back soon, for my heart yearns after her.'

Well, the stepmother and Long Leda set sail. They reached the prince's country without mishap, and Lilla Rosa received them graciously, glad to think that all the old enmity was now forgotten. But the prince, her husband, was not pleased to see them. He said to himself, 'No good will come of this!' He couldn't forget how cruelly the stepmother had treated Lilla Rosa; and as to Long Leda, she was so hideous that he couldn't bear to look at her. She was always scowling; but that was because she dared not laugh, lest a toad jump out of her mouth.

So, when the stepmother said that she and Long Leda must now be going home, the prince bade them goodbye with a cheerful heart. The stepmother said nothing about taking Lilla Rosa back with them to visit the king her father; *that* wasn't part of her plan! But before she went she took Lilla Rosa up to her room, and said, 'Dear little daughter, I have a gift for you, sent by your father.' And she took from its wrappings the beautiful robe of many-coloured silk embroidered with gold.

'Oh, how pretty!' Lilla Rosa said she would wear the robe that very evening, to surprise the prince. And the stepmother laughed and said, 'Yes, I'm sure he will be surprised!' And then she and Long Leda went to their ship and sailed away.

That same evening Lilla Rosa took the robe, held it up before her in front of a long mirror, and smiled to see how beautifully the many-coloured silk shone, and how the gold embroidery glittered. But then it seemed to her that there came a little sighing whisper that said, 'No, no, Lilla Rosa, don't put it on!' And so she stood for a moment doubtful. And then she thought, 'Bah! I mustn't be silly – this is a present from my dear father!' And she drew the robe over her head. . . .

Ah me, what happened? Lilla Rosa disappeared, and there in front of the mirror stood a great golden goose. And the golden goose gave a wailing cry, and flew out of the open window.

From that hour the linden ceased its playing, and the song of the nightingale was heard no more.

The prince, distracted with grief, sought for Lilla Rosa high and low. His people tried to comfort him, saying that Lilla Rosa must have gone with her stepmother and Long Leda to visit the king, her father. But the prince said, 'She would not do that without telling me.'

He wept, and would not be comforted. And as to Lilla Rosa's little son, he cried and cried.

Now on a calm night of full moon, when one of the prince's fishermen was out at sea, he saw a great golden bird swimming towards him on the path of the moon. All amazed – for he had never before seen a bird so beautiful – he rested on his oars gazing at it, almost holding his breath, lest he scare it away.

But the great golden bird didn't seem at all scared; it swam close up to the side of the boat, and then it spoke. Yes, it spoke in a human voice. And this is what it said:

> *'Good evening, fisherman.*
> *How are things at home in the royal palace?*
> *Does my linden play?*
> *Does my nightingale sing?*
> *Does my little son laugh by night and by day?*
> *Does my lord always make himself merry?'*

And, as if in a dream, the fisherman answered:

> *'At home, in the royal palace it goes ill.*
> *Thy linden plays not,*
> *Thy nightingale sings not,*
> *Thy little son weeps both by night and by day,*
> *Thy lord never makes himself merry.'*

The beautiful golden goose sighed, and said:

> *'Poor me!*
> *Who now float on the blue waves,*
> *And never more can be what I have been.*
> *Good night, fisherman.*
> *I will come twice more, and then never again.'*

Then the bird swam away. And the fisherman, greatly troubled, rowed to shore, hurried to the prince, and told him what he had seen and heard.

The prince said, 'If you will catch that bird and bring it to me, I will make you rich for life.'

So, next evening, the fisherman took a net and rowed out to where he had seen the golden bird. The night was dark. For a time he looked this way and that over the water, and saw nothing. But then the moon rose and lit the waves, and in the path of the moon came the great golden bird, swimming towards him. The bird came to the side of the boat, and said, as it had said the night before:

'Good evening, fisherman.
How are things at home in the royal palace?
Does my linden play?
Does my nightingale sing?
Does my little son laugh by night and by day?
Does my lord always make himself merry?'

And the fisherman answered:

'At home, in the royal palace it goes ill.
Thy linden plays not,
Thy nightingale sings not,
Thy little son weeps both by night and by day,
Thy lord never makes himself merry.'

Then the great golden bird spoke again:

'Poor me!
Who now float on the blue waves,
And never more can be what I have been.
Good night, fisherman.
I will come once more, and then never again.'

And it was about to swim away when the fisherman leaned from the boat and cast his net over it.

Then the bird beat fiercely with its wings and screamed, 'Let go quickly, or hold fast!' And at the same moment changed itself into a great serpent.

And the serpent writhed and twisted and beat upon the net. The fisherman was terrified, but he held on to the net with all his might. The serpent lashed the net this way and that, but still the fisherman held on, and still the serpent hissed and writhed and screamed, 'Let go quickly or hold fast'; and all at once it changed itself into a huge fire-spitting dragon and burst through the net, which so terrified the fisherman that he made haste back to shore, and ran to tell the prince.

The prince said, 'Tomorrow I will come with you; for catch that bird I must and will.'

So on the next evening he went with the fisherman upon the sea, and waited for the moon to rise. But black, wind-driven clouds covered the sky, the prince could hardly see a yard in front of him, and the boat was tossed this way and that on the blustering waves.

'My prince, had we not better row home?' said the fisherman.

But the prince said, 'No, no, no!' And all at once the clouds parted, the moon shone out, and swimming towards them, now on the crest of a wave, now in the hollow, came the great golden bird.

The bird swam up close to the boat and spoke:

> *'Good evening, fisherman, good evening, my prince!*
> *How are things at home in the royal palace?*
> *Does my linden play?*
> *Does my nightingale sing?*
> *Does my little son laugh both by night and by day?*
> *Does my lord always make himself merry?'*

And the prince answered:

> *'At home in the royal palace it goes ill.*
> *Thy linden plays not,*
> *Thy nightingale sings not,*
> *Thy little son weeps both by night and by day,*
> *And I, thy lord, never make myself merry.'*

The beautiful golden bird sighed and appeared very sorrowful, and said:

> *'Poor me!*
> *Who now float on the blue waves,*
> *And never more can be what I have been.*
> *Good night, fisherman; good night, my lord.*
> *Now I come hither never more.'*

The golden bird was about to swim away, but the prince leaned from the boat and caught her in his arms. And she screamed and struggled and beat with her wings and cried out, 'Let go quickly, or hold fast! Let go quickly or hold fast!' And turned at once from a golden bird into an enormous serpent. The serpent writhed and

twisted and tried to slip out of the prince's arms, but he held it
fast.

And it thrust its fangs into his arm and lashed him with its tail,
and screamed again, 'Let go quickly, or hold fast!' And all at once
changed itself into a monstrous dragon, whose flaming mouth
spat fire into the prince's face.

'My prince, my prince,' cried the terrified fisherman, 'let the
thing go!'

But the prince wouldn't let the dragon go, he clung on all the
harder.

And the dragon roared out, 'Let go quickly, or hold fast! Let go quickly or hold fast!' – and turned itself into a huge vulture that beat with its wings and pecked with its fierce beak, and tore the prince's hair out by the roots. The prince shut his eyes and turned his face away, but he gripped that vulture with all his might. And it screamed again, 'Let go quickly, or hold fast!' and turned itself into a great golden stag, that prodded with its horns and kicked with its feet. But still the prince held on.

Into furious shape after furious shape that creature changed itself, and still it struggled and screamed, 'Let go quickly, or hold fast!' and still the prince held on. Shuddering, half fainting, and drawing his breath in great gasps, he clung to the thing that fought and kicked and bit and scratched and hissed and spat: until with one last great cry, it lay still in his arms. . . .

And the being that the prince now clasped in his arms was his own dear wife, his beloved Lilla Rosa.

So he wrapped her in his mantle, and the fisherman rowed them home.

Now the story draws to a close, for there is little more to tell.

Next day the prince and Lilla Rosa and their little son took ship and set out to visit the king, Lilla Rosa's father. And when the ship came to land, and the stepmother saw who they were that stepped out of it, she gripped Long Leda by the arm, and together they stole out of the palace and fled away. Where they went nobody knew; and certainly nobody cared.

The old king was overjoyed to see his Lilla Rosa again, for the stepmother had reported her dead. So, after a long and happy visit, the prince and Lilla Rosa and their little son went home again to their own country.

And there the linden tree plays, and the nightingale sings; there Lilla Rosa's little son laughs both by night and by day; and there the prince at all times makes himself merry.

5 · Eh! Eh! Tralala!

An old man had a little cock with a golden comb; and he also had a clever little cat with green eyes. And one morning he said to the clever little cat, 'Puss, my dear, today I'm going into the forest to fell some trees for our landlord. You must cook me a nice dinner and bring it into the forest at midday; and Little Peter Cock shall stay and mind the house.'

Then the old man took his axe and his saw and walked off into the forest. Clever Little Cat Green Eyes stoked up the fire, and baked a meat pie. Little Peter Cock, who was rather lazy, sat perched on a chair back, watched Little Cat Green Eyes, and crowed:

'Cock-a-doodle-doodle-do!
Oh, what a busy little girl are you!'

So, when the pie was nicely cooked, Little Cat Green Eyes took it out of the oven, put it in a basket, and said, 'Peter Cock, now I'm off. Shut the window and lock the door behind me. *Stay in the kitchen*, don't go out, lest Slippery Fox come prowling, and snatch you up, and carry you away.'

'Trust me!' said Little Peter Cock.

'Well, I hope I can trust you,' said Little Cat Green Eyes. And off she went with the basket.

Little Peter Cock locked the door, Little Peter Cock shut the window, Little Peter Cock gobbled up a piece of pie crust that Little Cat Green Eyes had left for him. He flapped his wings, and strutted about the kitchen. 'This is very boring,' said Little Peter Cock. 'Why couldn't *I* have gone to the forest with that meat pie? But there – Master doesn't trust me, and Little Cat Green Eyes doesn't trust me. I am a very ill-used bird!'

And he sulked.

Then came Slippery Fox peeping through the window. And Slippery Fox began to sing:

> *'Kee-oo, kee-oo, anyone at home?*
> *Kee-oo, Peter Cock with the Golden Comb!*
> *Open the window, if you please*
> *And I will give you some nice green peas.'*

'Green peas, did you say?' cried Little Peter Cock. 'Yes, yes, I like green peas!'

And he opened the window, and put his head out.

Snap! Slippery Fox caught hold of Little Peter Cock's head, dragged him out of the open window, and ran off with him.

Then Peter Cock began to scream, 'Little Cat, Little Cat Green Eyes, Slippery Fox is carrying me away! He is carrying me along the road, and over the fields, beyond the dark forest, behind the high mountains, to a foreign land, to the ends of the earth! Little Cat Green Eyes, help! Help! Help!'

Little Cat Green Eyes was coming back from the forest. She heard Peter Cock's screams. She ran, ran, ran. She caught up with Slippery Fox. She pounced. She bit Slippery Fox on the side of his neck. Slippery Fox opened his mouth, he dropped Peter Cock, and scampered away.

Little Peter Cock lay on the ground with his eyes shut; he thought he was dead. But Little Cat Green Eyes picked him up, gave him a shake, and carried him home.

Next morning the old man went again into the forest; and again Little Cat Green Eyes cooked a nice dinner, and put the dinner in a basket to carry it to her master in the forest. And before she went, she said, 'Now Peter Cock, remember: *a locked door and a fast-closed window*, and neither door nor window to be opened until I come back.'

'Oh, I'll remember this time!' said Peter Cock.

'Well, I hope you will!' said Little Cat Green Eyes. And off she went with the basket.

She hadn't been gone long, when there came Slippery Fox again, prowling outside the window. And Slippery Fox began to sing:

> '*Kee-oo, kee-oo, anyone at home?*
> *Kee-oo, Peter Cock with the golden comb!*
> *Kee-oo, pretty orange nose,*
> *Kee-oo, pretty yellow toes,*
> *I've brought you beans, and I've brought you fish,*
> *Served up together in a pretty little dish.*'

'I don't believe you've brought me anything of the sort!' said Peter Cock. And he hopped on to the window sill, turned his head sideways, and peered through the pane with one eye.

Well, to be sure, Slippery Fox had *something* in his mouth; but Peter Cock couldn't see just what it was. So he opened the window and leaned out.

But all that Slippery Fox had in his mouth was an old saucepan lid. *Clitter clatter!* He dropped the lid. *Snap!* He caught hold of Peter Cock, dragged him out of the window, and carried him away.

Then Peter Cock began to scream, 'Little Cat, Little Cat Green Eyes, Slippery Fox has got me again! He is carrying me away, along the road, and over the fields, beyond the dark forest, behind the high mountains, to a foreign land, to the ends of the earth! Little Cat Green Eyes, help! Help! Help!'

Little Cat Green Eyes was coming back from the forest. She heard Peter Cock's screams. She ran, ran, ran. She caught up with Slippery Fox. She pounced, she bit Slippery Fox on the neck.

Slippery Fox opened his mouth in a howl, he dropped Peter Cock, he scampered away. Little Cat Green Eyes picked up Peter Cock and carried him home.

'R-*row*, r-*row*, r-*row*, you stupid thing!' Little Cat Green Eyes shook Peter Cock till his beak rattled. 'Will you never learn sense?'

Peter Cock didn't answer. He sulked, he felt very ill-treated, what with Slippery Fox deceiving him, and Little Cat Green Eyes scolding him. He turned his back on Little Cat Green Eyes, and began preening his rumpled feathers.

Next morning the old man went as usual to work in the forest. And as usual Little Cat Green Eyes cooked him a nice dinner, put the dinner in a basket, and set off to carry it to the old man. And before she went she said to Peter Cock, 'Now, listen to me! Today our master will be working deeper in the forest – a long way from here. If you are so silly as to let Slippery Fox carry you off, though you scream louder than loud, I shan't hear you. I shall be too far away. Now, I've warned you!'

Then off went Little Cat Green Eyes, carrying the basket. And Peter Cock locked the door, and shut the window.

Then came Slippery Fox singing outside the window. This time he was singing about roast chestnuts: a whole bag full of roast chestnuts he said he had brought for Peter Cock. Ah! Peter Cock did like roast chestnuts! But he wasn't going to open the window, not he! Slippery Fox sang his song about roast chestnuts again and again. But Peter Cock sat on a chair back, and preened his wings. . . . Oh dear me, Peter Cock's mouth began to water – but no, *he wasn't going to open the window*!

So at last Slippery Fox stopped singing. 'I don't think Peter Cock can be at home this morning,' said he. 'I think he must have gone into the forest with Little Cat Green Eyes. I shan't wait any longer. But I'll leave this bag of chestnuts here under the window for him to find when he comes back.'

Then Slippery Fox tiptoed away round the corner of the house, and hid.

Peter Cock flapped his wings and jumped off the chair back. He hopped on to the window sill, turned his head sideways, and peered through the pane with one eye. No Slippery Fox to be seen! But had he really gone home, or was he just hiding round the corner?

'I must make sure about that!' said Peter Cock. And he opened the window and put his head out.

Snip, snap! Slippery Fox leaped from behind the corner of the house, snatched up Peter Cock, and carried him off.

'Help! Help! Help!' Peter Cock was screaming for Little Cat Green Eyes, just as he had screamed yesterday, just as he had screamed the day before yesterday. But Little Cat Green Eyes was far away, deep in the forest. She didn't hear Peter Cock's screams. And Slippery Fox carried Peter Cock away to his house under the hill.

By and by Little Cat Green Eyes comes home, and the old man comes home. Where's Peter Cock got to? Oh me – see the window is open; and see, here are some of Peter Cock's speckled feathers drifting in the breeze! Oh me, Slippery Fox must have carried off Peter Cock!

The old man mourned; Little Cat Green Eyes mourned. Clever Little Cat Green Eyes said, 'Master, if you will allow me, I will set out to rescue Peter Cock.'

'Yes, go, Little Cat, go, go, my dear! If you think you can manage it?'

'I can manage it,' said Little Cat Green Eyes. 'But first I must disguise myself.'

Then Little Cat Green Eyes tied a mask over her face, and dressed herself up. She put on a long striped coat, and a little fur cap, and little red boots. And she slung a guitar over one shoulder.

'Master,' said she, 'what do I look like now?'

'Little Cat Green Eyes, you look like a strolling minstrel.'

'Ha, ha!' said Little Cat Green Eyes. 'Then give me that great big strong leather sack you've got in the attic.'

The old man rummaged in his attic and found the great big strong leather sack. 'Here you are, Little Cat,' said he.

Then Little Cat Green Eyes rolled up the sack, tucked it under her arm and set off, skipping along the road at a great pace, till she came to the house of Slippery Fox.

And outside the house she unrolled the great big strong leather sack, laid it down, and began to stroll about, twanging on the guitar and singing:

> '*Eh, eh, tra-la-la!*
> *Here come I with my guitar!*
> *Fox has four little daughters, oh,*
> *And one little son called Pooloopko!*
>
> *Eh, eh, tra-la-la!*
> *Good little children, so they are,*
> *Come, come out, each pretty little dear,*
> *Sweetest music you shall hear,*
> *Hear me sing to my guitar,*
> *Eh, eh, tra-la-la!*'

Inside the house the fox children were listening.

'Papa,' said the eldest little fox child, 'I am going out to see who is singing so beautifully.'

'Well, run along then,' said Slippery Fox. 'But come back soon; we are going to kill and cook Peter Cock presently.'

So the eldest little fox child went out.

Oh, ho! Little Cat Green Eyes snatched her up, and stuffed her into the big strong leather sack.

Then Little Cat Green Eyes began to sing again:

> '*Eh, eh, tra-la-la,*
> *Hear come I with my guitar.*
> *Fox has three more daughters, oh,*
> *And one little son, called Pooloopko.*
>
> *Eh, eh, tra-la-lay,*
> *Come out, children, hear me play,*
> *Play and sing to my guitar,*
> *Eh, eh, tra-la-la!*'

'Oh, Papa,' said the second eldest little fox child. '*I* want to go out and see the minstrel!'

'Go, my dear,' said Slippery Fox. 'But don't be long.'

So the second fox child went out.

Oh, ho! Little Cat Green Eyes snatched her up, and stuffed her into the big strong leather sack.

Then Little Cat began to sing again: '*Eh, eh, tra-la-la!*'

Slippery Fox was pushing sticks into the fire to make the oven hot. He hadn't killed Little Cock yet, but he had him on the table with his feet tied together. Slippery Fox was laughing. 'Do you know why I'm stoking up the fire, Little Cock with the Golden Comb?'

'N-no,' sobbed Little Cock.

'To roast you, my dear, to roast you,' said Slippery Fox.

'*Eh, eh, tra-la-la!*' sang Little Cat Green Eyes outside the window.

'Oh, Papa, Papa,' said the third little fox child, 'do let me go out and see the minstrel! I think he sings even better than you do!'

'Go, go, my dear,' said Slippery Fox. 'But nobody sings better than I do.'

So the third little fox child ran out.

Slippery Fox began sharpening the carving knife. 'Little Cock with the Golden Comb,' said he, 'do you know why I'm sharpening this knife?'

'N-no,' wept Little Cock.

'To kill you, my dear, to kill you,' said Slippery Fox.

Meanwhile Little Cat Green Eyes had snatched up the third little fox child and stuffed her into the sack. Now Little Cat was singing again: '*Eh, eh, tra-la-la! . . .*'

'Put some more sticks on the fire – pile 'em up, pile 'em up!' said Slippery Fox to the fourth little fox child.

The fourth little fox child piled sticks on the fire till the flames flew up the chimney. And then she said, 'Papa, just let me go out and see the minstrel!'

'Go then, go,' said Slippery Fox, 'but come back quickly.'

So the fourth little fox child went out. Oh ho! Little Cat Green Eyes snatched her up, and stuffed her into the sack.

63

Now there was only one fox child, little boy Pooloopko, left in the kitchen.

The fire roared, the oven was getting red hot, Slippery Fox said to little boy Pooloopko, 'Go out, sonny. Tell your sisters to come in, or they will miss a fine sight; because now I'm going to kill Little Cock with the Golden Comb and put him in the oven.'

So little boy Pooloopko ran out.

Oh ho! Little Cat Green Eyes snatched him up, and stuffed him into the sack on top of his sisters.

Then Little Cat Green Eyes began to sing again:

> *'Eh, eh, tra-la-la,*
> *Five pretty children, here they are,*
> *Fox's four little daughters, oh,*
> *And his one little son called Pooloopko.*
> *Now there lacks but Fox papa*
> *To hear me sing to my guitar,*
> *Eh, eh, tra-la-la!'*

'Plague take those children!' said Slippery Fox. 'The minstrel must have put a spell on them, though he doesn't sing half as well as I do!'

And he hurried out to fetch the children.

Whop! Down came Little Cat's guitar on the head of Slippery Fox. Little Cat knocked Slippery Fox silly, and stuffed him into the sack along with the children.

Then she fastened up the mouth of the sack, and went into the kitchen, where Little Cock lay on the table with his feet tied together.

Little Cock was shedding tears; but he cheered up when he saw Little Cat Green Eyes.

'Oh, you stupid thing!' said Little Cat Green Eyes.

And she picked up the carving knife and cut the string from round Little Cock's legs.

Little Cock stood up stiffly. He wiped his eyes with a draggled wing, and gave a feeble crow. Then he hopped off the table and followed Little Cat Green Eyes out of the house. Little Cat Green

Eyes took the sack, and they set off for home. The sack was very heavy. Little Cat dragged it along the road, bump, bump, and Little Cock with the Golden Comb walked meekly by her side.

'The trouble I have with you!' said Little Cat to Little Cock. 'But there, I suppose you can't help being silly.'

'I won't be silly any more,' whimpered Little Cock with the Golden Comb.

'Oh *won't* you!' said Little Cat Green Eyes. 'But silly or no, I expect our master will be pleased to see you.'

The old man was indeed pleased to see Little Cock with the Golden Comb. He clapped his hands and said, 'Welcome home, poor silly Little Cock! But as for Pussy Green Eyes, she's worth her weight in gold, so she is . . .! And now, what are we to do with this sack full of foxes?'

'Take it into the forest and leave it there,' said Little Cat Green Eyes.

So that's what they did. They dragged the sack into the forest, dumped it down under a tree and left it.

Then they went home to supper.

Inside the sack Slippery Fox was gnawing and tearing. All the little fox children were gnawing and tearing. They tore their way out at last, and ran back to their house.

And Slippery Fox said, 'Let this be a lesson to you, my children. Beware, beware, and *evermore beware of Green-Eyed Cats*. But as far as I'm concerned, the old man can keep his stupid Little Cock with the Golden Comb. Catch me ever going near his house again!'

6 · The Small-tooth Dog

Once upon a time there was a rich merchant whose business took him travelling into many distant cities. And one day, as he was riding homeward, with his pockets stuffed with gold, he was set upon by thieves.

The merchant defended himself as well as he could; but he was one, and the thieves were many. They had already dragged him from his horse, and had him lying on the ground, bleeding from many wounds, when a great ugly small-tooth dog came leaping from behind the hedge. Bristling, growling, snarling, biting, the dog set upon the thieves with such ferocity that they all fled. Then the dog, taking a firm grip of the merchant's coat, carried him along the road to a large house; and the merchant's horse followed along the road behind them.

In that house, which was a rich and handsome one, the dog laid the merchant on a bed. And though there seemed to be no one but the dog in all that great house, some sort of people there must have been; for invisible hands dressed the merchant's wounds, and brought him food, and tended him until he was well enough to journey home.

Then the merchant, overcome with gratitude, asked the dog what reward he could offer him.

'I have many curious and precious things at home,' said the merchant, 'and I would refuse you none of them. Will you accept a fish that can speak twelve languages?'

'No,' said the dog, 'I will not.'

'Or a goose that lays golden eggs?'

'No,' said the dog, 'I will not.'

'Then will you accept a mirror in which you can see what anyone is thinking?'

'No,' said the dog, 'I will not.'

'Then what will you accept?' said the merchant. 'For something I must and will give you.'

'Oh, all right,' said the dog. 'Go home. In a week I will come and choose for myself a present that pleases me.'

Well, the merchant rode home; and a week later, sure enough, there was the great dog standing at the door.

The merchant sent a manservant to open the door. But the dog wouldn't come in.

The merchant sent a maidservant to the door. But no, the dog wouldn't come in.

The merchant went himself to the door. But the dog just stood and stared.

So at last the merchant sent his young daughter to the door; and she was frightened, because the dog was so very large, and so very ugly. But she spoke up politely, and said, 'If you please, my father would like you to come in and choose a present.'

And the great ugly dog wagged his tail, and curled his lips into a smile, showing all his small teeth, and said, '*You* are the present I choose! Jump on my back, and I will take you home.'

Oh me, the girl didn't want to go, but somehow she had to. She got on to the dog's back, and off he went at a great pace, mile after mile, until they reached the dog's house.

Well, as you know, it was a large and handsome house, and the dog was kind. He gave the girl everything she could possibly need, and did his best to amuse her. So for a month she bore up. But after that first month she began to mope and cry.

Said the dog, 'What are you crying for?'

Said the girl, 'Oh, I want to go home and see my father.'

'Well,' said the dog, 'if you will promise not to stay home for more than three days, I will take you. But first of all – what do you call me?'

'A great, ugly, small-tooth dog,' said she.

'Then,' said he, 'I will not let you go.'

At that she began to cry more pitifully than ever; and she cried all day and all night. So next morning the dog said, 'Very well, I *will* take you home. But, before we start, tell me what you call me.'

'Oh,' said she, 'I think your name must be Sweet-as-a-honeycomb.'

'Jump on my back,' said the dog. And he wagged his tail and curled up his lips in a smile.

So she jumped on his back, and away he went at a fine pace, running smoothly and easily for forty miles or more. And then they came to a stile.

And before getting over the stile, the dog made a pause, and said, 'Now, what do you call me?'

'Oh,' said the girl, all joyous to think she was nearing home, 'what should I call you, but what you are – a great, ugly small-tooth dog.'

The dog didn't say another word; he turned round and carried her back to his house.

Well, she sobbed and she cried; she was sobbing and crying for a whole week, and the dog was growling and going round with his tail between his legs. It got so miserable in that house that at last the dog said, 'Perhaps I will take you home. But first – what do you call me?'

'Swee-eeter-than-a-hon-honeycomb,' sobbed the girl.

'Jump on my back,' said the dog. And she jumped on his back, and off they went once more, she gripping hold of his rough coat, and he running smoothly and easily for some forty miles, till they came to the stile.

'Now what do you call me?' says the dog.

'Oh,' says she, 'I call you Sweet-as-a-honeycomb.'

Then the dog gave a jump over the stile, and they went on for more and more miles, and came to a second stile.

So, before getting over this second stile, the dog made a pause, and said, 'Now what do you call me?'

'A great ugly small-tooth dog,' said she, before she could stop herself.

So the dog didn't jump over the stile, he turned round and carried her back to his house.

My word, how the girl cried! And how the dog growled! He

left the girl to herself, and she was crying all the time, and going round all red-eyed and slobbery with tears. 'You look a sight,' said the dog, 'and I shan't come near you.' And he didn't go near her for days and days, until at last she ran to him, and put her hands together as if she was praying, and said very meekly, 'Please, dear dog, please, Sweet-as-a-honeycomb, *please* take me home!'

69

'Up on my back,' said the dog.

And she got up on his back, and they set off.

Well, they came to the first stile. And before jumping over it, the dog said, 'Now what do you call me?'

'Sweet-as-a-honeycomb,' whispered the girl.

So the dog got over the stile and ran on, mile after mile, and came to the second stile. And there he stopped and said, 'What do you call me now?'

'A great –' she began. Then she remembered. 'No, no, what should I call you, and what do I call you, but Sweet-as-a-honeycomb?'

So the dog jumped over the stile, and on they went, and on they went. The girl was trying to please him now, and was babbling out every sweet saying she could think of: 'good dog' and 'brave dog' and 'kind dog'; and the dog, proud and happy, was galloping along with his mouth open, and his tongue dripping, and his tail going wag, wag, wag, from east to west, and back from west to east.

And so they came to her father's house. And the dog stopped in front of the door.

'*Now*, what do you call me?' says he to the girl.

And the girl, all excited to think she would soon be rid of him, and safe in her own home again, began, 'A great big....' *Ugly* she was going to say, and the dog was turning round to take her back, but she caught hold of the door latch and clung to it. Then the dog gave her such a sad, sad look as cut her to the heart, and all at once she remembered how good and patient he had been with her, and she cried out, 'Sweeter-than-a-honeycomb, that's what I call you! Sweeter-than-a-honeycomb! And good and kind and handsome!'

Well, well, she thought that now surely the dog would have been content and galloped off and left her; but he did no such thing. He shook her off his back, he stood up on his hind legs; with his two front feet he pulled off his dog's head and tossed it high into the air; his rough hairy coat dropped from him, and there he stood, the handsomest young prince in all the world, and laughing at her.

'Oh!' she said. 'Oh!'

'You may well say "oh",' laughed he. 'But if I've been a trouble to you, it's nothing to the trouble you've been to me, and I thinking all the time that I should have to remain under a spell for the rest of my life! But come, let us go in to your father; and if he says yes, will you say yes, and marry me?'

'Oh *yes*!' said the girl.

And they both laughed.

Then hand in hand they went into the house, and the prince told the merchant how a witch had turned him into a dog, because he refused to marry her hag of a daughter. 'And a great ugly small-tooth dog you shall remain,' the witch had said, 'until some maiden calls you handsome. And bah! you hideous creature, that will never be!'

'And now, merchant,' said the prince, 'you once told me that your house contained many treasures, and you offered me my choice of them. So of all the precious things you possess, I choose for myself the most precious – your daughter to be my bride.'

'Oh, with all my heart!' said the merchant.

So the girl and the prince were married. And after the wedding the prince took his bride home to his grand house, where they were waited on now, not by invisible hands, but by rejoicing servants, from whom also the spell had been lifted.

And there they lived in happiness ever after.

7 · The Dolphin

I The Ring and the Princess

Once upon a time there lived a fisherman and his wife who were sorely grieved because they had no children. So the fisherman went to consult a wizard, and the wizard said, 'In the depths of ocean there swims the fish Deep Under. If you catch this fish and cook it, and if your wife eats of its liver, she will bear a child.'

The fisherman had never heard of the fish Deep Under; but he set out in search of it. He sailed over seven seas, he cast his net in deep waters and in shallow waters, in the day time, in the night time, in calm and in storm; he caught fishes big and fishes little, but he never caught Deep Under. And to everyone he met on his journeyings he put the same question: 'Can you tell me where Deep Under is to be found?' And from everyone he got the same answer: 'You are wasting your life. Go home! Neither hook nor net can reach so deep as the depths where Deep Under swims.'

So at last, sick at heart, the fisherman turned his boat and set sail for home. And there came a Dolphin swimming round the boat. And the Dolphin said, 'Fisherman, fisherman – why so sad?'

The fisherman told him, and the Dolphin said, 'I am the king of the dolphins and I can help you. I know where the fish Deep Under lurks, and I can bring it to you. But in return you must make me a promise. If, having eaten of Deep Under's liver, your wife should bear a son, give me your promise that I may be the child's godfather.'

'That I promise gladly,' said the fisherman.

The Dolphin said, 'Then wait for me in yonder little cove.' And he swam swiftly away.

The fisherman steered his boat into the little cove, let down his anchor, and waited. He waited one day, he waited two days, he waited three days, but never a sight did he get of the Dolphin.

'Bah! The creature was fooling me!' thinks he. 'I'm off home!' And he pulled up the anchor and was running up his sail when there came a flurry of waves, and there was the Dolphin bounding through the water faster than fast, with a little golden fish in his mouth.

'Here is Deep Under,' said the Dolphin, tossing the little golden fish into the boat. 'I have kept my word; do you keep yours, fisherman. Call me on the day of the christening.'

Then the Dolphin swam away, and the fisherman sailed home, with the little golden fish, Deep Under.

Well, his wife cooked and ate that little golden fish, and what do you think? By and by she gave birth not only to one baby but to a couple, a boy and a girl, as handsome a little pair of twins as you could find should you search the world over. The parents decided to call the girl Anna and the boy Peter. And now came the question of the christening.

Among the fisherfolk there were plenty who were willing to stand godparents; but our fisherman, mindful of his promise to the Dolphin, declared that the christening must take place on the sea beach, and for that the priest was not very willing. However it was that or nothing with the fisherman, so the priest had to agree. The christening party went down to the beach, and there was the Dolphin waiting.

The Dolphin said and did all that was required of him as well as any human godfather could have done; and before going back into the water he said to the fisherman, 'When your son is grown up, if ever he needs help, let him row out to sea and call me.'

Well, the twins, Peter and Anna, grew and flourished. They were handsome, they were happy, they were strong and good; they rejoiced the hearts of their parents. Anna worked about the cottage and garden with their mother; Peter went fishing with their father; and often as they sailed the deep waters, the fisherman would talk to Peter of his Dolphin godfather, and Peter would cast his eye over the sunlit or the starlit or the moonlit waters, hoping for a sight of that godfather, but never a sight did he get.

So life passed pleasantly for many years; but alas, when the twins were but scarce grown up, a fever struck their village, and both their parents caught the fever and died. Then Peter must go to sea alone to earn a livelihood for himself and Anna, who cooked and cared for him and washed and mended his clothes in loving and sisterly fashion.

Now on a hill above the fishing village stood the king's summer palace. The king was a widower, and he had an only daughter, the princess Nina, young, beautiful and good. There were suitors and more suitors – princes, dukes and lords – arriving every day at the palace with their gifts and proposals for the hand of princess Nina. But the king thought none of them good enough; he had made up his mind that Nina was to marry the Emperor of the East, and he got tired of being pestered by all these other suitors. So what did he do? He went sailing in the royal yacht, and in the middle of the Great Bay he took off his ruby ring and threw it into deep water. Then he went back to the palace and sent out heralds: 'Oyez, Oyez, Oyez! Somewhere in the waters of the Great Bay his majesty the king has lost his ruby ring. Whosoever can find the ring and restore it to his majesty within seven days from this day, shall have the princess Nina to wife and become heir to the throne. But whosoever tries to find the ring and fails, shall come no more within the king's presence on pain of death.'

'And so we get rid of these tiresome suitors,' thought the king with a chuckle. 'For of course they will all go seeking for the ring. And of course none of them will find it!'

Well, you may be sure that for the next seven days the Great Bay was crowded with all manner of boats, big and little; and all manner of men, young and old, rich and poor, were stripping off their clothes and diving down into the water, and coming up empty handed, and going down again, and yet again; whilst in the palace on the hill the king was sitting on a balcony watching the scene through a telescope, and chuckling.

But the lovely princess Nina ran to hide herself in her room, and there she drew the curtains across the window and sat on her bed and wept. She thought her father was making a fool of her, and though he had told her about the Emperor of the East, that didn't comfort her. She didn't want to marry any tiresome old emperor whom she had never set eyes on. She knew well enough whom she would like to marry, and that was the young fisherman, Peter, whom she sometimes met when he brought a basketful of fish up to the palace, and who was so strong and handsome, and who smiled so charmingly, and who walked as if he owned the world. But of course she couldn't tell the king – or anyone else – about Peter; and so, whilst the suitors dived, and the king, sitting on the palace balcony with a telescope to his eye, watched and chuckled, poor young princess Nina hid herself in her room and wept.

And what was our young fisherman Peter doing? Well, he was diving with the rest – for now it seemed that he had as good a chance of winning the princess as any prince or lord or duke among them all.

So one day passed, and another day passed, and still the Great Bay was crowded with boats big and little; and still from dawn to dusk, yes, and even by starlight, the divers were going down, and coming up with nothing better than a handful of sand or a pebble or two. But after the third day many gave up the search and sailed away, cursing the king for having made fools of them. And when the seventh day dawned none were left seeking but the local fishing lads, and even these, as that seventh day wore on towards sunset, hoisted their sails and returned to harbour.

Now the sun, lowering in the west, sent a glittering pathway across the quiet water, and in the stern of the boat stood fisherman Peter, silhouetted against the sun, cupping his hands to his mouth and calling loud, 'Godfather, godfather Dolphin!'

See – on the instant – there comes the Dolphin, rushing through the water. 'Godson, what do you wish?'

'Oh, godfather Dolphin, I would wish help in finding the king's ruby ring.'

'Godson, in a little minute, or in a long minute, I will find it.'

Down dives the Dolphin, up he comes again. Has he found the ring? No, he hasn't. He swims here, he swims there. He takes breath, down he goes again in another place. Up he comes again:

no ring yet, and the sun, a great red ball, rests on the horizon – the seventh day will soon be gone, and all Peter's hopes gone with it! What is Dolphin doing? He is resting on the water, he seems to be listening. Can he hear the ring calling? Who knows? But suddenly he swings round with a mighty splash, dives in another place, comes up, and in his mouth – see, *the ring*!

'Catch!' The ring, a tiny red flame, flashes from godfather Dolphin to godson Peter. 'Now be off with you, godson Peter, for you have no time to waste. But when next you need me, don't wait so long before you call. For if you call, I come. If you do not call – how should I come?'

Then, even whilst Peter was blurting out his thanks, the Dolphin swam away. And Peter rowed home. . . .

'Anna, sister Anna, I have the king's ruby ring! Bring me a clean shirt, bring me my Sunday suit, bring me one of your roses to wear in my buttonhole! And hurry, hurry, I must to the palace before nightfall. Oh dearest sister Anna, I feel my heart will burst with joy!'

Sister Anna hurried to fetch Peter his clean shirt and his Sunday suit, she cut a red rose and put it his buttonhole, but she was not smiling. 'Peter, dearest brother, hope little and expect less – the king is evil and hard of heart.'

'Anna, dearest sister, now unless I hope much and expect all, my heart will break.'

And so dressed in his Sunday suit, with a red rose in his button-hole and carrying the king's ruby ring wrapped in a clean handker-chief, Peter hurries to the palace, tells his errand, and is brought into the king's presence.

'Your majesty, I have brought you back your ruby ring.'

'Fisherman, I don't believe you. Let me see it! Bah, it must be a fake! Where was it found?'

'On the sea bottom, your majesty. How could I, a simple fisherman, contrive to fake such a ring as this?'

'Yes, yes, *you, a fisherman*, that's just the point. . . . Well, I will grant you that the ring is genuine, and your reward shall be a sack full of gold. . . . For you must see for yourself that it is impossible that *you – a fisherman –* should inherit the kingdom, and it is impossible that *you – a fisherman –* should marry my daughter. She herself would not hear of it!'

'If the princess might be asked about that, your majesty?'

'No, she shall *not* be asked!' The king flew into a temper, stamped, and began to shout. 'How dare you suggest such a thing? Be off, you ragamuffin! Get out of my sight! Don't you dare approach me again, until you come with a chest full to the brim with pearls and diamonds – and that will be never, never, never!'

Peter walked off with his head held high. He went down to the harbour. He stood on the edge of the starlit water; he cupped his hands before his mouth and called loud, loud, 'Godfather Dolphin!'

On the instant, there came the Dolphin, rushing through the star-streaked water.

'Godson, what do you wish?'

'Godfather Dolphin, the king has broken his word. It is not enough that I return his ruby ring. Now I must bring him a chest full to the brim with pearls and diamonds.'

'Godson, you shall carry him such a chest. At daybreak to-morrow, you will see in the Great Bay a small green boat, far out and gently rocking. Row to that little boat, tow it ashore, and take what is in it. And so, godson Peter, until we meet again, all good go with you!'

'And with you, godfather Dolphin.'

The Dolphin swam away. Peter went home. Before dawn next morning he was up and looking out over the Great Bay. Yes, there was the little green boat, far out and gently rocking. Peter took a tow line, ran his own boat down into the water, jumped in, and rowed to the little green boat. In the little green boat was a big chest of oakwood. Peter towed the green boat ashore, and lifted out the chest.

My word, but that chest was heavy! Peter could scarcely drag it home. And when he did get it home and lifted the lid – what did he see inside? Heap upon heap of sparkling diamonds, heap upon heap of shimmering pearls! Oh ho, faithless king, what will you make of this lot? For now here comes Peter again, a rope over either shoulder, toiling up the hill to the palace, dragging the oakwood chest on a handcart behind him.

The king, having breakfasted, is sunning himself on the terrace. When he sees Peter, he leaps up, shouting and stamping with rage. But Peter sets the chest before him, loosens the ropes, lifts the lid. Ah, ah! The diamonds sparkle, the pearls shimmer. The king plunges both hands into the chest. He would almost wish the

jewels to be fakes that he might get rid of Peter; but his greed exults to know that they are real.

'Rogue – where did you get them?'

'I found them in the Great Bay, your majesty.'

'You lie, you lie! You are a thief! You would swindle me with stolen goods! You deserve to be hanged, sir, yes, hanged! And if I spare your life, it is only that I am merciful by nature – but you shall do no more thieving!'

The king calls his guards. Peter is marched away to prison, in a great fortress that stands on a rock jutting out into the sea. And the king has the chest carried into his treasury and spends the morning gloating over the gleaming jewels.

But what now? Here is Peter's sister Anna at the palace doors, clamouring to be let in, clamouring to see the king and say her say in defence of Peter. But no, the king will not see her: she had better take herself off, or she will find herself in prison also. 'What, she won't go? Guards, put her outside the gates. Take a whip to her if need be. . . .'

So there goes Anna down the hill again weeping bitter tears. And weeping she comes to the fortress prison on its rock above the sea. She calls, calls, 'Peter, Peter, oh, my brother, my brother Peter!'

But the fortress walls are thick, he does not hear her. She flings herself down there on the rock, and weeps till dawn.

And in the dawn with the high tide comes the Dolphin.

'Dear, kind, loving Anna, why do you weep?'

'I weep because the king has shut Peter up in prison behind seven iron doors. Oh, good Dolphin, if you could but rescue Peter and win his princess for him, I would give you all the little I possess!'

'Would you give me yourself, Anna, to be my wife?'

'Yes, gladly, gladly!'

'Anna, I will set Peter free. Under the fortress there are deep sea caves, that the king's guards know nothing of. Through those caves I will bring Peter out. Now dry your eyes, go home, put your house in order, and prepare yourself for a long voyage. Tomorrow morning, when the tide is high, go down to the harbour. There you will find the princess. And what the princess asks you to do – that you must do. Goodbye till tomorrow, Anna.'

'Till tomorrow, Peter's godfather.'

The Dolphin swam away. Anna walked home. She set the house in order, tidied up the garden, made two small bundles of her own clothes and Peter's clothes, got through the day and the night somehow, and on the morrow's dawn, there she was, down in the harbour. The tide was full. Peter's little boat rocked gently in the shallows; and in the boat who should be sitting, elbow on knee, head in hand, but Princess Nina. And Princess Nina lifted her eyes to Anna, and said, 'Peter's sister, will you row me out into the bay for a little while? My heart is sorrowful and my head aches, and on the land I cannot rest.'

'Surely I will row you out, my princess.'

So Anna jumped into the boat, pulled up the anchor, took the oars, and rowed Princess Nina out into the still waters of the bay. And by and by Princess Nina leaned towards Anna and said, 'Peter's sister, now we are alone, quite, quite alone where no one can hear us, I have something to tell you. I love your brother Peter – oh how dearly I love him! – and now he is in prison for my sake, and my heart is breaking. If we cannot rescue him, I shall surely die.'

Anna looked over the calm water, 'Princess, *we* have no need to rescue him. See there – over there!'

Now the sun, risen behind the castle hill, threw a pathway of glittering gold across the still water; and in the golden pathway the Dolphin was swimming, carrying Peter on his back. And now Peter was in the boat, and one moment Anna was in his arms, and the next moment he was on his knees at the feet of the princess.

'Fisherman Peter, it was you who found my father's ring?'

'Yes, my princess.'

'Then fisherman Peter, why do you not claim your reward?'

'Oh, my princess!'

'Yes, *your* princess, Peter, now and forever.'

But the Dolphin was beating the water with his tail. 'Come, come, this is no time for dallying. Hoist the sail, godson Peter; the wind is scant enough, and we have a long way to go.'

'Where are we going, godfather Dolphin?'

> *'Across the sea*
> *There to live free.*
> *Now follow me.'*

So Peter hoisted the sail and took the helm and the Dolphin swam ahead, leading the way. All day they sailed, south by west, came at evening to the shore of a new country, and landed at the quay of a small fishing town, where the people were friendly and welcomed them with few questions asked.

In that town, as soon as might be, Peter and the princess were married. And after the wedding the Dolphin gave Peter a small bag of pearls and said, 'Godson Peter, go sell these pearls, and buy yourself a cottage and any fishing gear you need, that you may earn a living for your wife and yourself. As for me and my bride, we must go to my kingdom under the sea.'

Then the Dolphin took Anna on his back, and set off to swim to his own kingdom. And Peter and the princess stood on the sea beach and waved to them until they were out of sight.

II Anna, the Dolphin's Wife

For seven days and seven nights the Dolphin swam over the deep sea with Anna on his back, and came at last to the entrance of a cave on a great island.

Then the Dolphin said, 'Anna, my wife, under this island lies my kingdom. What will it please you to do? Will you live in your maiden shape on the island, or will you take dolphin shape and swim down with me into my kingdom?'

Anna said, 'I will be as you are, my husband.'

Then the Dolphin gave a heave of his back and tossed Anna high into the air. *Wh-hish!* Up she went. *Splish-splash!* Down she fell into the sea. And as she touched the water – there she was, no maiden any more, but a dolphin. And merrily, merrily the two dolphins dived down into the cave and swam out through the cave into the depths of ocean.

Now dark and ever darker grew the depths they swam through; and now dolphin Anna could see nothing, and must be guided only by her husband Dolphin's voice, until, away in the distance, shimmered a little gleam of light. And as they swam towards that shimmer of light it grew brighter and brighter and bigger and bigger. Now it was not one light but many lights, lamps innumerable, golden, glowing, lighting up a great city, whose inhabitants, big and little, came swimming out to meet the two dolphins, hailing them as king and queen.

So, amid a hubbub of cheering and splashing and echoing voices, King Dolphin and Queen Anna were escorted by their rejoicing subjects to the royal palace. And Queen Anna said, 'If all now goes well with my brother Peter, the world can hold no happier soul than I.'

Now you will remember that at parting the Dolphin had given Peter a little bag of pearls, and told him to sell them. Well, Peter did that, and with the money he got for them he bought a cottage close to the harbour, and also nets and lines and all the fishing gear he needed. Every day now he put out to sea with the other fishermen and did well enough; though he might have done better if Princess Nina had had any ideas about housekeeping. But she hadn't. She couldn't resist buying pretty things when she saw them, and so some of their money was wasted on useless trifles. But, bless me, what did that matter to either of them? They had enough to eat, and they loved each other – and what more did either of them want? If only, ah, if only they could have been left in peace!

But far away across the sea, in his palace on the hill, the king,

Princess Nina's father, was flying into one rage after another, and sending out ships all over the world to search for the princess. The ships were laden with pretty and costly goods, and the crews had orders to trade as merchants in any country they might reach, and never to cease from searching until they found the princess. For the ship's crew who found her and brought her home there awaited a big reward; for the ships' crews who returned before she was found there awaited the gallows.

So at last it happened that one of these ships came into the harbour of the very fishing town where Peter and Princess Nina were living; and the captain and the first mate strolled into a quayside tavern to glean what news they might.

In the tavern they met two fishermen; and then it was drinks all round and, 'What news, my lads?' And they soon learned all about Peter and his beautiful wife, who was such a careless housekeeper and so fond of pretty things.

The captain winked at the first mate, the first mate winked at the captain. The captain said, 'The lady sounds like a customer for us. We are merchants who deal in pretty things. Now, my lads, there are three pieces of gold waiting for all or any of you who will bring the lady on board our vessel that she may see our goods. What – her fisherman husband might object? Then wait until he's out at sea, and then bring her. Is that a bargain?'

Oh yes, to be sure, it's a bargain; since three pieces of gold don't come so pat into a man's hand every day!

So, next morning, after Peter has set out for the fishing grounds, and Princess Nina has watched his little boat until it disappears round the cliffs beyond the town, and has then gone back into the cottage and shut the door – *rat-a-tat-tat!* Somebody knocking! And she opens the door again.

'What, fishermen Tom and Dick – not at sea yet? My Peter's been gone this half hour! *What* do you say? You are messengers from two merchants who have pretty things to sell? You think I would like to see them? Well, so I would ... but as to buying, I don't know ... but there, it costs nothing to look. ... Yes, I'll come with you. ...'

And she goes.

The captain receives her with bows and smiles. He leads her down into the cabin where all the pretty things – coloured silks and satins and jewelled ornaments – are laid out for her to see. Meanwhile Tom and Dick have each been given their three gold pieces and gone. . . .

And after that?

Well, after that, it's up anchor and put to sea, my lads, as quickly and quietly as may be; and the princess, absorbed in all the pretty trifles the captain is showing her, notices nothing until the ship begins to heave under her feet. What's this? She flings down the jewelled comb she is trying in her hair, runs up on deck, sees the shore, the town, the harbour, her own cottage drawing every minute farther and farther away, rushes down to the cabin again.

'Captain, what is the meaning of this? Take me back to land *at once!*'

'Your royal highness, it grieves me to have to disobey you, but I have come by the order of the king your father to bring you home.'

'Home! My home is over there, in that little white cottage near the harbour wall. Oh, captain, have pity! Take me back! I have never done you any harm – why must you break my heart? Think of my poor husband – oh me, what will become of him? Take me back, take me back!'

All no good: orders are orders and must be obeyed, so the captain tells her. And when she tries to throw herself overboard then the captain, very regretfully, very politely, ties her hands together and her feet together, and lays her on cushions on the cabin floor. . . .

So when Peter came home that evening he found the cottage empty. Where could Nina be? It wasn't like her not to be waiting to greet him. He strolled into the town, seeking her. Not finding her he began to feel anxious. 'Has anyone seen my wife?' Yes, a woman had seen her in the morning going down to the harbour with two fishermen. What two fishermen? Well, Dick and Tom. Where are they now? Well, in the tavern. So to the tavern runs

Peter, and finds Tom and Dick in merry mood, having parted with one of their gold coins.

'*What have you done with my wife?*'

'Done with her? We ain't done nothing with her, nor to her. We took her down to a ship to see some wares.'

'What ship?'

'The big trading ship in the harbour.'

'*There is no big trading ship in the harbour!*'

'Well then, it must have gone.'

Ah me – yes, it must have gone.

Peter went back to his empty cottage and wept. . . .

III The White Ship

And far away in his kingdom under the sea the King Dolphin said to his dolphin wife, Anna, 'I have a feeling that all is not right with my godson, your brother Peter. At the moment I cannot leave my kingdom, so you had better go and visit him.'

Dolphin Anna set off swimming. She swam for seven days and seven nights, and came to the fishing town, and found Peter lying face downward on the sand.

'Peter, brother Peter!'

No answer.

Dolphin Anna poked him with her nose and flapped him with her flippers and Peter shrugged up one shoulder and said, 'Leave me alone!'

But dolphin Anna wouldn't leave him alone. She kept poking him. 'Brother Peter, tell me, only tell me what is the matter! Have you and Nina quarrelled?'

Peter sat up then, he looked wild. 'Ah! Ah!' he cried. 'If we could but quarrel! But the king has sent a ship. They have taken her away. I shall never see her again. Never, never! And now I shall die!'

But dolphin Anna said, 'For shame! I will return to my Dolphin king, your godfather. He will tell us what to do. Keep up your heart! We will get Nina back!'

And she went down into the sea and swam away, and came after seven days and seven nights to the dolphin kingdom, and told King Dolphin all that had happened.

King Dolphin said, 'This is a bad affair. In order to win back Peter's wife, my Anna, I must turn you once more into a human maiden. But if I do that, will you ever come back to me?'

And Anna answered, 'Of course I will come back to you, my husband! This is now my life, and I would not change it for all the world.'

So they swam up through the cave together. And King Dolphin seized dolphin Anna in his mouth and flung her high into the air. *Wh-hish!* Up she went. *Splish-splash!* Down she fell. She went up a dolphin; she came down a maiden. And King Dolphin took her on his back, and swam for seven days and seven nights, and came to where Peter paced the shore under his cottage in a frenzy of impatience and grief.

'Godson,' said King Dolphin, 'I fear you are neither calm nor sensible.'

'Godfather,' said Peter, 'how can I be calm, how can I be sensible, dallying here and doing nothing? Set me but doing something and I will be as calm as Anna here, and sensible as yourself.'

'Then, godson,' said the Dolphin, 'run your boat down into the sea, and row out with Anna to the place that I shall show you.'

So Peter launched his boat, and he and Anna got into her, and Peter took the oars and the Dolphin swam ahead, leading them along the coast and into a cove that Peter had never seen before. And in the cove was anchored the most beautiful white ship that anyone ever saw, with silver sails and gold masts and rigging, and a crew of smart lads in green jackets piped with silver. At sight of Peter the crew raised a loud cheer; and a company of elegantly dressed lords and ladies came to lean over the rails and join in the cheering.

'This is your ship, godson Peter,' said the Dolphin. 'And in it you will sail to your old home, where the king now holds your wife, the princess Nina, a prisoner. But the rescuing of the princess is your sister Anna's affair, not yours, and what she tells you to do, that you must do. Now get aboard your ship, and be off.'

Then the Dolphin swam away, and Peter and Anna went aboard the white ship. A troop of ladies-in-waiting led Anna below and clothed her in silk and velvet and set jewels in her hair and diamonds about her throat. And when they had done with her she came laughing to Peter and said, 'Please to remember that for the time I am not your sister Anna, but the Princess Anyetta, an emperor's daughter, and so, Captain Peter, you must obey me in all things.'

And Peter laughed and said, 'At your orders, my princess!'

So they sailed to the land where they were born, and when they came in sight of the king's palace on the hill, Anna said, 'Now, Captain Peter, get you below, and stay below, until I bring your wife to you. And whether that will be in a short time, or a long time, I cannot tell.'

So Peter went below, and the first mate steered the white ship into the harbour, and Anna disembarked, followed by a train of lords and ladies, and was carried in a litter up to the king's palace, where she had herself announced as Princess Anyetta, the daughter of the Emperor of the Seven Kingdoms, and now on her travels to see the world.

The silly old king was delighted to receive the emperor's daughter; and he ordered the best rooms in the palace to be got ready for herself and her attendants. He also sent a message up to Nina, who was moping in her own room, ordering her to come down *at once* to welcome the Princess Anyetta.

Nina came, proud and cold. But when she saw Anna she gave such a start as nearly gave the game away. And then she laughed and kissed Anna on both cheeks, and said, 'You are welcome, Princess Anyetta.'

The foolish king was delighted, and thought, 'That's all Nina wants – a companion of her own age.' And he said, 'Most beautiful Princess Anyetta, would it please you to stay in my kingdom for a while?'

And Anna answered, 'I will look round. If what I see pleases me, I will stay. If not, I will leave tomorrow morning.'

Well, it seemed that what she saw didn't please this haughty princess, because next morning she told the king that she intended to travel on. But first she invited the king and Princess Nina to visit her ship. 'We will hold a little feast in pledge of our good will,' said she, 'for it is right that we should part friends.'

Well, well, the king was disappointed that she was going so soon, but he was delighted to visit the ship. He was shown all over it by the first mate, the captain being 'indisposed and confined to his cabin – strictly by my orders,' explained Princess Anyetta. And this was true enough, because she had actually locked Peter up in his cabin, lest he give the game away by rushing to embrace his wife.

Fortunately the king was too busy admiring the beautiful little ship to bother about the captain. And as to the feast – the delicious foods and the rare wines – well, by the time all that was swallowed down, the king was in no mood to think of anything but the charms of his hostess. He even found himself proposing to her; but she laughed and told him she was already engaged.

'And now we must part,' said she when the feast was over. 'And I hope we part good friends?'

The king said it was impossible they should part otherwise. He made a little speech: Both he and his daughter Nina, he began. Then he looked round. It seemed that Nina was no longer with them. Where was she? Did anyone know? Yes, a little page knew. The Princess Nina had told him some time ago that she was going home.

'*Going home!* And without a word to our hostess! What manners! What terrible manners!' The king couldn't apologise humbly enough to his beautiful hostess. And he rode off up to his palace determined to give Nina a good talking to. . . . But first he called for his telescope and sat on the balcony to watch the wonderful white ship hoist her silver sails and put out to sea.

It was not until the ship had rounded the western arm of the Great Bay and was out of sight that the king laid aside the telescope, frowned, stalked indoors, and sent a lady-in-waiting to summon the Princess Nina.

The lady-in-waiting was gone a long time. She came back at last to say that the Princess Nina was not in her room.

'Then find her, find her!' said the king.

The lady-in-waiting went; she was gone for a longer time. When she came back it was to say that she couldn't find the Princess, nor could anyone tell her where she was. But on a table in her bedroom was a sealed letter which had been lying there since early this morning. And this letter she now handed to the king.

The king broke the seal and read:

'Papa,
I am going home to my dear husband, fisherman Peter. What is done is done. You cannot undo it. So please be sensible and leave us alone.

> Your daughter,
> Nina.'

Cannot undo it indeed! He both could and would! In a temper terrible to see, the king ordered out the largest of his fighting ships, got aboard, and set out in pursuit. . . . And he hadn't been long at sea before a storm blew up. Huge black clouds darkened the sky, monstrous waves tossed the ship this way and that, and flung their spume in the king's face.

'Your majesty,' said the captain, 'There is mischief brewing: the sky becomes blacker and ever blacker, we had best turn back.'

Turn back! What next? The king wouldn't hear of it. . . .

'Majesty, this is no ordinary storm. Devils howl in the rigging. Indeed, indeed we had best turn back.'

'Cowardly fool! Sail on!'

'Majesty, the waves beat higher and higher. They come against us like an army on the march, they rise against us like a host of phantoms, they shout and scream and menace us, calling, "Turn back"!'

But the king still shouted, 'Sail on!'

'Majesty, see how the lightning flames all about us! Hark, hark how the thunder cracks and roars! Such a storm I have never known before – if we don't turn back we are lost!'

'Dastard, poltroon, chicken-livered milksop! If you dare to turn back I will have you hanged!'

Flash after flash of lightning, peal after peal of thunder, one moment in blinding light, the next moment in pitchy darkness, amid monstrous waves the ship was rolling, heaving, shuddering, wallowing, until suddenly, with a leap like a bucking mule, she cracked in two: the king was flung in a high arc over the waves, and into the waves, and under the waves . . . and felt something beneath him give a heave and raise him again to the surface. Where was he? Seated on King Dolphin's back, whilst here, there and everywhere around him swam other dolphins picking up the drowning crew from amidst the wreckage.

Now the Dolphin began to speak: it was one king speaking to another. 'I am King of the Dolphins. Listen to me. Peter the fisherman is my godson. He brought your ring from the depths of the sea. You broke your word, denying him your daughter. You demanded a chest full of jewels. He brought you the jewels. Again you broke your word, denying him your daughter and flinging him into prison. With my help he escaped from prison and won his bride. What next? You stole his young wife from him, and came near to breaking two loving hearts. Do you now deserve that I should rescue you and carry you home?'

'No,' shivered the king. 'I-I can't say that I deserve it.'

'Yet I will carry you home on one condition,' said the Dolphin, 'that you will leave my godson and his wife in peace.'

'I will leave them in peace,' shivered the king. 'I repent me of my wicked ways.'

So then the Dolphin swam back to land with the king, and all round him swam his subject dolphins carrying the captain and crew of the king's ship.

The rescuing of the king and the ship's company by a shoal of dolphins was a marvel that the king's people have talked of from that day to this. So now we will leave them talking, and go to see how it fares with the voyagers in the white ship. Certainly they met no storm on their voyage home, for the Dolphin saw to it that they left the storm behind them. And they came safely into the cove where Peter had first found the white ship.

Then Peter and his sister Anna and his wife, the Princess Nina, disembarked, and the white ship with its silver sails and golden rigging put to sea again. The crew of smart lads in green jackets piped with silver raised a cheer, and the company of elegantly dressed lords and ladies leaned over the rails and waved their handkerchiefs. And Peter and Anna and the Princess Nina waved back, and watched the white ship out of sight. But to what port that white ship was now bound they did not know, nor can I tell you.

All I can tell you is that no sooner was the white ship out of sight than Peter and the Princess Nina found themselves in Peter's little fishing boat, sailing home to their own cottage.

Now Anna was left alone. She stood on the edge of the water and heard a voice calling, 'Anna, my wife, Anna!'

'I am here waiting for you, my husband.'

'Anna, is it happier on the dry land or in the deep water?'

'It is happier where you are, my husband.'

'Then come to me, Anna.'

Anna waded out into the sea. She waded out up to her armpits, and there was King Dolphin swimming to meet her. King Dolphin took Anna on his back, and tossed her high into the air. *Wh-hish!* Up she went. *Splish-splash!* Down she fell into the sea. And as she touched the water there she was, not a woman any more, but a gentle, lustrous-eyed dolphin.

And merrily, merrily, the two dolphins swam away together to their kingdom under the sea.

8 · Little Barbette

There was once a young widow who had a little daughter called Barbette. The widow's father was a rich nobleman who possessed a stately manor house, a farm, a mill, a bakehouse, a stable full of fine horses, many oxen, a big herd of cows, and a great flock of sheep. So, whilst this nobleman lived, the widow and little Barbette were well provided for. But when the nobleman died – oh dear, what happened? The nobleman had made no will, and he had three rascally brothers who seized his property and divided it between themselves.

The eldest brother, Perik, took the manor house, the farm, and the horses.

The second brother, Robardic, took the mill and the herd of cows.

The third brother, Duval, took the oxen, the bakehouse, and the flock of sheep.

So what was left for the widow and little Barbette? Only a leaky turf hut on the edge of a barren moor. And if the widow's greedy uncles could have thought of any other use for the hut, they wouldn't even have let her have that.

Now in the hut the young widow must sit and spin all day, earning just enough to keep herself and Barbette from starving. But they were soon both of them in rags. Not that it mattered to little Barbette, who wandered on the moor collecting the prickly furze for firewood, and saving the crumbs from her breakfast bread to give to the birds that sang among the bushes.

There was one robin who was Barbette's particular friend. He came to meet her every morning, and followed her about, perching on this bush and that bush, opening his beak wide, wide, and singing with all his might.

'Oh, Robin,' said Barbette one morning, 'I wish I knew what

you were saying! For I think you are trying to tell me something.'

Robin flew down from bush to ground. He cocked his eye at something that glittered there. Barbette thought the glittering something was a coin, and she picked it up. But it wasn't a coin; it was a golden pebble.

It was indeed a magic pebble, and it gave to whomsoever held it the power of understanding the language of birds and beasts. So now Barbette could understand what Robin was saying.

'Barbette! Barbette!' sang Robin. 'Come with me! I've something to show you, come with me, come with me, little Barbette!'

Barbette flung down the bundle of furze she had gathered, and followed Robin, who flitted before her over the moor, and across fields, and up on to a range of sandhills. Then he came to flutter over Barbette's head. 'What do you see down there, down there?' says he.

'I see down there the ocean, calm as a lake. And on the ocean I see seven islands shining in the sun.'

'And do you see something lying down there, down there on the shore, Barbette?'

'Yes, I see a pair of wooden shoes lying there, and also a holly staff.'

'Come down on to the seashore then, little Barbette. Put on the wooden shoes, and take the holly staff in your hand.'

So Barbette followed Robin down to the seashore, put on the wooden shoes, and took the holly staff in her hand.

And Robin said, 'Now you will walk across the sea to the first of the seven islands. You will go round the island until you find a rock on which a sea-green rush is growing.'

'And what shall I do then, dear Robin?'

'You will pluck the rush and use it for a halter.'

'And what shall I do after that, dear Robin?'

'You will strike the rock with the holly staff: the rock will open, and a cow will come out of it. You will put the halter round the cow's neck, and you will lead her home, little Barbette.'

Well, Barbette, wearing the wooden shoes and holding the holly staff, stepped into the water. *Into* the water, did I say? No, *on to* the water: for there she was, walking over the sea, light and easy as you please, and so came to the island. She went round the island, and found the rock with the green rush growing on it. She picked the rush, she struck the rock with her holly staff: the rock opened, and out came a great cow, with gentle eyes and a coat that shone like satin.

Little Barbette put the rush round the cow's neck for a halter, and led it back over the sea, without either of them so much as wetting their feet.

Robin had flown away. Barbette took off the wooden shoes, laid them with the holly staff where she had found them. Then she led the cow home to her mother.

Ah, how Barbette's mother laughed and clapped her hands when she saw that beautiful sleek and shining cow! 'Now you shall have all the milk you can drink, my little Barbette!' said she.

And she fetched a pail and a stool, and sat down to milk the cow.

My goodness gracious, there seemed to be no end to the milk that cow gave! It flowed like water from a spring. The milk filled every pail and every pitcher, and every pan and every bowl the widow possessed, and still it flowed. Little Barbette hurried away into the village to borrow more pails. The milk filled every vessel Barbette could bring, and still it flowed and flowed.

The villagers came crowding; they stood staring and gaping. Whoever asked for milk got milk free, and still the cow gave more and more. Only when every vessel was full, and everyone's thirst was quenched, did that milk cease to flow.

'Have you seen the widow's magic cow? Have you *seen* it?' Everyone was chattering; the fame of that cow spread far and wide. Farmers came wanting to buy, offering fistfuls of gold, bidding one against the other. But no, the widow wouldn't sell, not she!

Then came the widow's eldest uncle, Perik, and said, 'Blood is thicker than water. You are my niece. You can't refuse to sell *me* the cow.'

Oh, couldn't she? She could, and she did.

'I will give you all my horses,' said Perik. But the widow didn't want his horses.

'I will give you my farm,' said Perik. But the widow didn't want his farm.

'Well then,' cries Perik at last, 'I will give you the manor house – the house of your father, where you were born.'

And the widow, because she loved her father's house, said, 'Yes, it is a bargain, take the cow.'

So Perik led the cow away to his farm, and the widow and little Barbette went to live at the manor.

The widow was happy to be home again, but Barbette wouldn't be comforted. She wanted her magic cow. She cried all day, and cried herself to sleep that night. . . .

'Barbette! Barbette!' Now it was morning, and someone was calling her. Barbette sat up in bed, rubbed her eyes. There was Robin perched on the bed rail.

'Little Barbette, come out, come out!' sang Robin. 'And bring your golden pebble. I've something to show you, something to show you, little Barbette!'

Little Barbette jumped out of bed. She took the golden pebble from under her pillow and ran out, just as she was, in her night-gown. Robin flew across the manor court to the stables, and Barbette pattered after him on her bare feet.

'Open the stable door!' sang Robin.

'But there's nothing in the stables,' said Barbette. 'Great-uncle Perik has all the horses.'

'Open the door! Open the door!' sang Robin.

So little Barbette opened the stable door. What did she see in there? The magic cow!

'Oh, my cow, my darling big cow, who brought you back?'

'I brought myself back,' said the cow. 'I wasn't going to live with that mean Perik creature.'

'Oh, but my cow, he won't let you stay. He'll come and fetch you away!'

'He may come, but he won't fetch me away, little Barbette. Now, take your magic pebble in your hand. Stroke me with it three times from head to tail, and say three times:

95

'Magic stone and magic sea,
Change my magic cow for me.'

Well, Barbette did that. What happened? The magic cow disappeared; and there in its place stood a great dappled horse, whose coat shone like satin, and whose mane and tail shone like silver.

'Oh, oh, my horse, my darling big horse!'

'Go and dress,' said the horse, 'and I'll take you for a ride.'

Who was happy now but our little Barbette? She spent the day in the manor fields, perched on the back of the great dappled horse who carried her so lightly, so smoothly, that it was like flying through the air. Yesterday she had gone to bed crying; today she went to bed laughing, and dreamed that her horse had wings, and that they were indeed flying through the air.

But in the morning her mother said, 'We have corn to sell. We will send our horse to market with as many sacks as he can conveniently carry.'

So the manor servants brought out the corn sacks, and began loading up the horse. Did you ever? The more sacks they loaded on to his back, the bigger and stronger grew that horse; he became a giant of a horse; the servants had to fetch a ladder to reach up to his back, and still they piled on sacks, and still he grew and grew, until there was no more corn for him to carry.

So away with him to market, and the town in an uproar, everyone running and shouting, 'See, see the widow's horse! The horse! The horse! See, see the widow's horse!'

And as it had been with the cow, so it was with the horse. Everyone who had money enough was wanting to buy it. But no, the widow wouldn't sell, not she!

Then came the widow's second uncle, Robardic, with the same old tale of blood being thicker than water; and offering this, offering that, in exchange for the horse. But no, the widow wouldn't sell. Until at last Robardic offered her his mill and his herd of cows.

And the widow said, 'Yes, these things were my father's. I should like to possess them.'

So she took possession of the mill and the herd of cows, and Robardic led away the dappled horse, whose coat shone like satin, and whose mane and tail shone like silver; and who, with every corn sack that was taken from his back, had lessened in size, until he was now no bigger than he had been when Barbette first saw him.

Barbette shed a tear or two when she saw the horse led away. But Robin came to perch on her shoulder and whispered in her ear, 'Dry your eyes, little Barbette, your horse will come back to you.'

And in the evening, sure enough, there was the horse back in the manor stables.

'Oh, my horse, my darling big horse!' Little Barbette clapped her hands and jumped for joy.

'That's all very well,' said the horse, 'and I'm glad to be back. But hurry now: we've work to do, or that mean greedy Robardic will be after me again. Take your magic pebble, stroke me with it three times from mane to tail, and say three times:

> *'Magic stone and magic sea,*
> *Change my magic horse for me.'*

Barbette did that. The horse disappeared; and in its place stood a great ram with golden horns, and white fleece soft as new fallen snow, curling thick over his back and reaching to the ground.

'Oh, oh, my ram, my darling ram!'

Barbette ran to fetch her mother. Her mother came and said, 'Fetch me the clippers, little Barbette; the poor creature is all but smothered in that heavy fleece.'

Barbette fetched the clippers, the widow began to shear the ram. Did you ever? As the fleece fell, so it grew again, till the widow stood knee deep in the snowy white wool.

'Barbette, Barbette!' said the widow. 'This one ram is worth all the flocks in the country!'

So everyone thought; and it wasn't long before the widow was being offered gold and more gold for the sale of the ram. But to all who came bargaining the widow said, 'What do I want with your gold? I am in no need. I have my father's manor, my father's mill, and my father's herd of cows – go away!'

But at last came the widow's third uncle, Duval, carrying a heavy purse. 'Blood is thicker than water,' said he. 'I am your father's brother; here is gold – sell me the ram!'

The widow said, 'I do not want your gold.'

Then Duval cried out, 'I will give you my oxen, my bakehouse, and my flock of sheep.'

And the widow answered, 'Because these things were my father's, I should like to possess them. Take the ram.'

Duval led the ram away in triumph. It didn't trouble him that he had parted with so much of his property. He still had a cottage, and he was going to make his fortune with the ram – oh, wasn't he just! He was chuckling to himself, he felt like dancing, as he led the ram away to his cottage.

Now the road to his cottage lay along the edge of the sea, and as they came near the shore, the ram gave a hop, a skip, and a tug. He broke the rope that held him, and scampered off across the sands. Duval raced after him, swearing and shouting. But the ram plunged into the sea and swam to the nearest island. And on the island the rocks opened to let him in, and closed again behind him.

Yes, the ram was gone; Duval might stamp and scream and shout himself hoarse; he might even plunge into the sea and try to swim to the island – it was all no good; the waves rose up and tossed him back to shore. And he went away to his cottage, dripping wet and howling with rage.

That evening Barbette went to the stable to look for the ram. She felt certain he would come back, just as the cow and the horse had come back. And, sure enough, there he was.

'Oh, oh, my ram, my darling big ram!'

'That's all very fine,' said the ram, 'and it's nice to see you again. But I've had a troublesome day, and I'm tired of all this chopping and changing. Now I've come back, I intend to *stay* back. So take your magic pebble, stroke me with it three times from horns to tail, and say three times:

> '*Magic stone and magic sea,*
> *Change my magic ram for me.*'

Barbette did that. What happened? The ram disappeared, and there in its place stood a smooth spotted dog, with one blue eye and one brown eye, and a wisp of a tail curled over his back.

'Oh, oh, my dog, my darling spotted dog, don't ever leave me!'

'I don't intend ever to leave you, little Barbette,' said the smooth spotted dog. 'I don't think anyone will want to buy *me* in a hurry. Why should they? I'm no beauty!'

'I think you're the loveliest thing in all the world,' said little Barbette. 'Except Robin, of course. Robin, Robin – where are you?'

Little Barbette ran out of the stable with the smooth spotted dog at her heels. Robin was perched on a paling.

'Well, little Barbette, are you happy now?'

'Oh, Robin, I couldn't be happier!'

'Glad to hear it,' said Robin. 'You're a very lucky girl, Barbette. So long as you have your magic pebble, all the animals and birds will be your friends. The birds will sing to you, and the animals will talk to you, and you will understand everything they say. But don't you ever forget, Barbette, that it was *I* who found the magic pebble for you.'

'I will never forget it,' said Barbette.

Then Robin puffed out his little chest, opened wide his little beak, and sang and sang.

He was immensely proud of himself.

9 · Jon and his Brothers

Well, there was a poor man – a widower – and he had three sons. Antoine was the eldest, Andrew came next, and Jon was the youngest. They were good lads, all three.

Well, these three lads grew up, and the poor man, their father, died. So then Antoine said, 'Brothers, there is not much for us' here; I will go out into the world and seek my fortune.'

So he got ready to set out; and before he went he filled a glass with clear water, set it on the kitchen table and said, 'Brothers, every day you must take a look at the water in this glass. As long as the water remains clear, you will know that all is well with me. If the water turns muddy you will know that I am in trouble, and then you, Andrew, must seek me out and aid me. But if the water turns black, you need not trouble yourselves about me any more, because I shall be dead.'

So having said, Antoine took a loaf of black bread and a staff of blackthorn, and set out.

Every day Andrew and Jon looked at the glass of water. And for maybe a week, or maybe longer, the water was clear as crystal. But one morning Jon, who had risen early, came running to wake Andrew, crying out, 'Brother, brother, the water in the glass is turning muddy! Oh, now Antoine must be in trouble!'

Andrew jumped out of bed and ran into the kitchen. There was the glass standing on the table; and even as he looked at it, the water became darker and darker. Now it was almost black. Oh me, Antoine must be in deadly peril!

So Andrew snatched up a loaf of black bread and a staff of blackthorn, and set out to look for Antoine. But before he went he took another glass, filled it with clear water, set it on the kitchen table, and said to Jon, 'Brother, watch this glass. If the water remains clear, you will know that all is well with me; if it becomes muddy you will know that I am in trouble, and then, Jon, you must seek me out and aid me. But if the water turns black, do not trouble yourself any more about me, but live in happiness, because I shall be dead. So now goodbye, brother.'

And so having said, Andrew set out, hurrying along the road which Antoine had taken before him.

Every morning after that, Jon looked at the two glasses. The water in Antoine's glass remained dark, but it never turned quite black, so Jon knew that Antoine must be still alive. And for a week or so the water in Andrew's glass stayed clear as crystal, so Jon knew that all must be well with him. But one evening, before going to bed, Jon looked at the glasses again, and the water in Andrew's glass was whirling round and round as if someone was stirring it up with a spoon, and every moment it was becoming darker and darker.

Jon didn't wait for morning; he snatched up a loaf of black bread and a staff of blackthorn, and hurried out along the road which his brothers had taken. And walking fast, almost running, he covered many miles before sunrise. Now he was meeting many people, for it was market day in a nearby town; and of everyone he met, Jon asked the same question: 'Have you by chance seen a young fellow, or maybe two young fellows, wearing grey jerkins, each carrying a blackthorn staff like mine, and walking this way?'

But nobody had.

So he went, went, went, walking straight on, for many days, asking everyone he met for news of his brothers, getting no news, but saying to himself, 'No, they are not dead, they cannot be dead, and some day I shall find them!'

And then one day he overtook a merry party of people old and young, going along the road, laughing and singing. And he asked of them the same question: 'Have you seen a young fellow, or two young fellows, walking this way, wearing grey jerkins, and carrying blackthorn staffs like mine?'

Oh no, they hadn't seen anyone like that! They told Jon that they had been at a wedding, and they were now going back with the newly married pair to a little feast in their village. And they said, 'We are going your way, so come, join us, join us, for it is well known that a stranger brings luck to the newly wed.'

Well, Jon was very hungry, for he had long ago eaten his loaf of bread to the last crumb, and he had no money to buy another. So he went with them and got a good meal, and stood up with the rest to drink the health of the bride and bridegroom. And then he said he must be getting along, and the bridegroom said, 'Before we part we must give you a present – what shall it be?'

And Jon answered, 'Oh, just some small thing. A good piece of cord would do nicely.'

The bridegroom said, '*A piece of cord!* No, no, you're joking!'

And Jon said, 'Indeed I'm not joking. I will fasten the cord round my waist in memory of all you kind people.'

Well, since he would take nothing else, Jon got his piece of cord, tied it round his waist, bade goodbye to the merry wedding party, and walked on.

It was springtime, the birds were mating and building their nests, and it seemed that human beings must have the same idea, for Jon hadn't been walking for many days when he overtook another merry wedding party. And they too invited Jon to come with them and share the wedding feast. Jon went willingly enough, and filled himself up with good food and drink, and again was asked to say what he would choose as a parting gift.

Jon said, 'Well, I would like this napkin.'

What, a grubby little soiled napkin! Oh no, no, no, Jon must have something better than that!

But Jon said yes, yes, yes, that was all he wanted. So they gave him the napkin, and he wished them joy, and went on his way.

He went, went, went, asking everyone he met for news of his brothers, and getting none. And one day – did you ever? – he overtook yet a third wedding party, and walked on with them to share their wedding feast. The feast was in a barn, for the people were humble people, and the barn was lit up with candles. So, when the feast was over, and the bridegroom asked Jon to choose a parting gift, Jon took up a burnt down candle-end and said, 'This is the gift I choose.'

A candle-end – what use was that to anyone? Oh no, Jon must choose something else! But Jon wouldn't choose anything else; and after a lot of laughing and protesting, he got his candle-end, wished the bride and bridegroom joy, and went on his way.

Well, he went, went, went on a long lonely road. He went for a week without meeting anyone. He slept under hedges, and pulled up and ate a turnip or two from the fields as he passed – for surely no one would begrudge a poor hungry fellow a turnip! And at the end of a week, as he was going along munching his turnip, he saw an old grey horse standing by the side of the road.

And the old grey horse said, 'Hullo, Jon!'

'Hullo to you!' said Jon. 'But that's funny – you can speak, and you know my name!'

'Of course I can speak,' said the old grey horse. 'And I know you very well, Jon. So, if you'll get up on my back, I'll ease your legs from walking.'

'And they need easing too,' said Jon. 'Thank you very kindly!'

And he scrambled up on to the horse's back.

The old grey horse set off at a brisk pace. And by and by he said, 'Jon, I know you're looking for your brothers, and if you follow my advice, I promise you that you'll find them. For they are not dead, you can rest assured of that. But now listen to me carefully. Very soon we shall be coming to a castle where the witch maidens live. They will invite you in to eat and drink with them, and of course you are hungry. *But do not eat, do not drink,* or you will bitterly rue it. Are you going to take my advice, Jon?'

'Well,' said Jon, 'you seem such a knowing old fellow that I expect I'd better.'

'Indeed and indeed you'd better, Jon,' said the old grey horse.

So they went along, and they went along, and by and by they came to a great castle with a roof covered with gold tiles. And there, standing at the castle gate, were three most lovely witch maidens.

'Oh, poor tired traveller!' cried the witch maidens. 'Come into our castle, and we will give you food and drink.'

'I don't think I can spare the time, thanking you kindly,' said Jon.

But the grey horse whispered, 'Go in with them, Jon, but take nothing to eat and nothing to drink.'

So Jon slid off the horse's back and went into the castle with the witch maidens.

The witch maidens brought him into a banqueting hall. In the hall there were many other witch maidens, sitting round a table, where a feast was spread. And, 'Eat, dear Jon,' they said. And 'Drink, dear Jon,' they said.

But Jon answered, 'Thank you, gentle maidens, but I have already dined.'

'Then pledge us in a glass of wine, dear Jon,' said the witch maidens.

But Jon answered, 'Thank you, gentle maidens, but in the forest I passed by a fountain, and there I quenched my thirst.'

'But just to drink to our good healths, dear Jon!' said the witch maidens. 'You can't refuse to do that!' And they filled a glass with wine that sparkled ruby red, and held it out to Jon.

'I wish you good healths with all my heart,' said Jon. 'But drink I cannot.'

Well, they urged him and urged him, and still Jon said no, and no, and no. And at last those witch maidens became very angry, said he was an unmannerly boor, and that unmannerly boors must die. And they dragged him out to hang him from a tree in front of the castle gate.

But they had no cord. Then they saw the cord that Jon had been given by the first wedding party, and which he had tied round his waist. And they took that cord, and made a noose of it, and put Jon's head in the noose, and hung him up, and went away. But, wonder of wonders! – that cord lengthened itself and lengthened itself, until there was Jon standing on the ground. And the old grey horse, who was waiting outside the gate, called out, 'Quick, Jon, cut the cord!'

So Jon took his jack-knife out of his pocket and cut the cord, and laughed, and said, 'What next?'

And the grey horse said, 'Go into the witch maidens' garden. In the garden you will find a flower bed, and in the middle of the flower bed stands a tree. The tree has three branches, and on one branch grow three golden apples. Pick those apples and bring them here. But hurry, Jon, hurry; for if the witch maidens see you, you are lost.'

So Jon ran into the garden, and found the tree with the three branches and the three golden apples. And he picked the apples and brought them to the horse.

'Good, Jon, good! That was well done,' said the horse. 'And now we will begin by destroying this castle and the wicked witch maidens.'

'But, my good horse – how can we do that?'

'Throw one apple on to the golden tiles of the castle roof, Jon.'

So Jon threw an apple on to the golden roof, and – *boom bang! boom bang!* – the earth under the castle opened; down sank the castle and all who were within it, walls and windows, doors and chimneys, slowly slowly sinking, till only a last gleaming fragment of the tallest golden chimney could be seen. Next moment that too disappeared; and the earth closed over it.

'Now we must ride for our lives,' said the grey horse. 'Up with you, Jon!'

One leap, Jon was up on the grey horse, and off they went, galloping, galloping, galloping.

But not all the witch maidens had gone back into the castle after they thought to have hung up our Jon. Some of them had gone picking berries in a nearby wood, and as Jon and the grey horse were galloping past this wood, the witch maidens spied them, and screaming with rage, rushed out of the wood in pursuit.

The grey horse was going fast, but the witch maidens were going faster, they were fairly whizzing along, going so fast that their feet seemed scarcely to touch the ground. Yes, they were gaining on Jon and the horse: and now in front of Jon and the horse stretched a vast lake, with no way over it, and no way round it.

'Oh me!' cried Jon. 'We are lost!'

'Not yet, Jon,' said the grey horse. 'Throw an apple into the lake.'

Well, Jon did that. What happened? The lake disappeared, and there where it had been was a great plain covered with growing corn.

Over the plain and through the corn galloped Jon and the grey horse. And over the plain and through the corn the witch maidens rushed to follow them. But though the plain stretched wide and firm under the horse's hoofs, behind the horse the lake re-formed, wide as the world and deep as the pit; and screaming and struggling, the witch maidens sank down and down and down – and the waters closed over their heads.

'Hurrah!' cried Jon.

'I don't know that it is hurrah yet,' said the grey horse. 'On this journey it seems that trouble must follow trouble.'

And the grey horse was right; for there was one witch maiden who had not run with her sisters out of the wood, but had lingered there to fill her basket. And even one witch maiden can make trouble enough in the world, heaven knows!

However, for the time all went well. The grey horse and Jon crossed the plain in safety; and here before them was a broad high road that led to the city of a king.

'But, oh, my dear horse,' said Jon, 'my stomach is crying out for food!'

'Well then,' says the grey horse, 'we'll stop here. Off my back with you, Jon, and spread the little napkin you got from the second wedding party.'

'*What!*' says Jon. 'You know about that!'

'I know about many things, Jon,' said the old grey horse.

So Jon got down and sat by the side of the road, took the napkin out of his pocket and spread it. Did you ever? There on the napkin was food and drink, good food and plenty of it, and a beaker full of wine; and beside the napkin stood a bucket full of water and a goodly pile of oats and bran.

'Oh ho, my horse, oh ho!' says Jon. 'Now we will make merry!'

So they ate and drank. And when they were satisfied, what was left of the food, and the empty wine beaker, and the water bucket all disappeared. So Jon folded up the napkin and put it back in his pocket.

Now it was night, and they both lay down and slept.

In the morning Jon spread the napkin again, and they got a good breakfast. And after that they rode on again, cheerily, cheerily, and came into the king's city, and rode through the city to the gates of the king's palace. And there, in front of the gates – what did they see? A beautiful girl buried up to the neck in sand.

Jon jumped down and ran to her. He began scooping up the sand with his two hands, but as soon as he scooped up one handful, another handful took its place, and dig as he might the beautiful girl stayed buried up to the neck.

'Oh me!' cried Jon. 'What is to be done?'

'Dear kind lad,' said the beautiful girl, 'there is nothing to be done. This is the witch maidens' work, and they are all-powerful. So go your ways, kind lad, and leave me to my fate.'

'But – but –' cried Jon, 'the witch maidens are all dead, drowned in deep waters – we saw it happen, my horse and I!'

Then a smile lit up the girl's face; and if she had been beautiful in her sorrow, she was beyond all things beautiful in her joy. 'Dead! Are they indeed dead?' she cried. 'Then, oh then I am free!'

And she rose up out of the sand as far as her ankles: but do what she would, she could not get her feet clear.

'Oh me!' she cried. 'I am not free after all! It cannot be that all the witch maidens are dead!'

'Whoever is dead and whoever is alive,' shouted Jon, 'you shall not stay here!' And he clasped his arms about her, gave a mighty heave, and lifted her clear.

Then she shook the sand from her garments, and stood before Jon, laughing and radiant.

'Now I will go to my father, the king,' she said. 'Come again tomorrow and the king will reward you.'

'I am not seeking reward,' said Jon.

'Nevertheless you shall have it,' said she, and went from him in
through the palace gates. And it seemed to Jon that his heart went
with her.

'Jon,' said the old grey horse, 'I think we are nearing our
journey's end.'

'Not so,' said Jon. 'I have still to find my brothers.'

'If you will do what I ask you, Jon, you shall find them
tomorrow,' said the horse.

'Then of course I will do what you ask,' said Jon.

'Is that a promise, Jon?'

'Yes, it is a promise, my horse.'

That night Jon and the grey horse slept in a nearby wood, and
next morning, Jon, all eager, hurried back to the palace. But he
found guards set at the gates, and the guards refused to let him
in. They told him they had strict orders to admit no one.

'What's to be done now?' says Jon to the old grey horse.

'There's much to be done,' said the horse. 'You see yonder fig tree?'

'Yes, I see it.'

'Then take your last golden apple and throw it up into the tree,' said the horse.

Well, Jon did that. And immediately a golden axe fell down from the tree.

'Pick up that axe, Jon,' said the old grey horse.

Jon picked it up.

'Is the edge of the axe sharp, Jon?'

'Yes, it is very sharp, my horse.'

'Then give it a swing, Jon, and cut off my head at one blow.'

'Oh no, my horse, no, no, *no*!'

The horse gave a stamp, and his eyes flashed with anger.

'What did you promise, Jon. Wasn't it to obey me in all things?'

'Yes, but – oh, my dear horse!'

But the more Jon protested that he couldn't and wouldn't do it, the angrier grew the horse. He said he would gallop away out of Jon's life forever. He said that Jon would never find his brothers, he stamped and scolded, and showed his teeth, until at last in desperation Jon swung the axe. *Chop* – off flew the head.

'Oh me, what have I done?' Jon shut his eyes and put his two hands before his face; he fell on his knees and wept.

'Jon, Jon, look up, Jon!'

Whose voices? His brothers' voices! And there indeed were his brothers, Antoine and Andrew, lifting him to his feet, hugging him, calling him by dear names, and crying out, 'The old grey horse has kept his promise, Jon, for we were that old grey horse.'

Then they told him how it had all happened. First Antoine in his travels had come to the witch maidens' castle, and eating and drinking with them, had been put under a spell, so that he could not leave them. Then Andrew, in search of Antoine, had come to the castle, and was told that Antoine was inside; and so, all eager, he too had gone in, and found Antoine, and feasted with the witch maidens. And so as the brothers sat side by side, full of meat and drink and as happy as could be, the lovely laughing witch maidens had said, 'Would you like to see us work some magic?'

'Oh yes!' said Antoine.

And, 'Oh yes!' said Andrew.

And scarcely were the words out of their mouths before the witch maidens came crowding round them, touching them with their white hands, and crooning such a magic sleepy song that they both fell asleep. And when they woke – ah me! – now there was no Antoine, there was no Andrew, only a bony old grey horse. And the witch maidens took whips and drove the horse out of the castle to wander whither he would.

'And I don't know how it came about, Jon,' said Antoine, 'that we were changed into one shape and not into two. But it seemed that just as we fell asleep, we gripped each other by the hand. And since the witch maidens couldn't loose our hands, because of the brotherliness between us, they had to change us both into the one shape. . . . And so wandering in bitter despair for days and days, that old grey horse at last met with their brother Jon, coming to seek them. . . . And the rest you know, Jon, the rest you know! But come now, we will all three go to the king's palace and tell our story.'

So they went to the palace; but the guard who stood at the gate drew his sword and said, 'What do you want?'

'To see the king, whose daughter we saved,' said Jon.

'What – *you*!' said the guard.

'Yes, we,' said Jon. 'And if you can't let us in without permission, then go and ask the king.'

The guard went grumbling. He soon came back, and several more guards came with him. And the guards seized Jon and Antoine and Andrew, and dragged them off and flung them into a den where the king kept wild beasts – lions and tigers and bears and wolves.

Well, well, that was something that shouldn't have happened. And it wouldn't have happened if all the witch maidens had been drowned in the lake. But you will remember that one of them was not drowned, because she had stayed behind in the wood to fill up her basket with berries. And it was this witch maiden who, following after Jon in a furious rage, came to the king's palace, disguised herself as a courtly dame, and told the king that she, and she alone, had lifted the princess out of the sand. The poor young princess couldn't deny it, because the witch maiden put yet another spell upon her – a spell that made her forget Jon altogether.

And the king, in his joy and gratitude, said to the disguised witch maiden, 'For this I will make you my queen!'

So now we have the palace a-bustle with preparations for a grand wedding, the witch maiden triumphant, the princess in an unhappy daze about everything that had happened, and Jon and his two brothers flung into the wild beasts' den.

In the den the lions were roaring, the tigers were spitting, the bears were growling, and the wolves were howling. And though, outside, the sun had but just set, in the den it was already pitch dark. But Jon still had the candle-end that he had been given by the third wedding party, and he took the candle-end out of his pocket and lit it.

I tell you, the flame of that candle flared up and shone like the very sun, and so great was its brilliance that the wild beasts, all amazed, fell silent and slunk into corners. And Jon laughed and said, 'Now the company shall dine!'

So he spread his little napkin, and got a splendid dinner for himself and his brothers; and what's more, he got a great dish of food for each of the animals. Then everyone ate until they were satisfied; and after that they all lay down and slept.

So day followed day, and it might have been worse. The candle-end gave all the light they needed, and the napkin gave them food in abundance. The animals grew tame as great dogs, and fond of all three brothers, but fondest of Jon who fed them. But the brothers became very bored, and often and often they made plans for escape; but the walls of the den were thick and strong – there seemed no way of breaking through them. And often and often, too, Jon thought of the lovely young princess, and mourned to think that perhaps he would never see her again.

But 'never', Jon, is a long word. And if by chopping off the letter with which that word begins, we do not make it any shorter, we do at least make it more hopeful. And Jon did see his princess again; and this is the way it came about.

On a calm summer evening, one of the king's guardsmen was taking a stroll through the palace grounds, and he passed near to the wild beasts' den. Now though the sun had set it was not yet dark in the grounds; but in the wild beasts' den it should, of course, have been blacker than black. So what was the guard's astonishment to see a brilliant ray of light that shot up through a grating, gilding here a tree and there a bush with a golden glow, and rising in radiance even to the very clouds.

The guard, almost scared out of his wits, ran to tell the king. The king ordered out a company of soldiers, and putting himself at their head – for he was no coward – went to the den, and ordered the heavy trap door to be swung open.

What did the king see when he peered through the trap door? He saw Jon's lighted candle-end balanced on a broken bucket, shooting out its brilliant rays in all directions. And he saw, gathered round the broken bucket, a merry company: Jon, Antoine, Andrew, lions, tigers, bears, wolves and all, seated at supper. And such a supper! For each man and beast had the food he liked best.

The king, almost gibbering with astonishment, ordered the three prisoners to be let out, and listened without a word to Jon's long story of how it all happened. He called for the princess, and she came; and when she saw Jon the spell was lifted from her memory, and she ran to him, crying out, 'This is he who delivered me out of the earth, this is he whom I love – oh, my dear, my dear – how could I have forgotten you?'

So they all went back to the palace together. The king ordered the witch maiden to be thrown to the wild beasts, and they had no scruple about tearing *her* up! And the king said, 'I am a stupid old widower, but you, Jon, shall marry the princess and be my heir – that is if you are willing?'

Jon was more than willing: it seemed to him as if he had left the earth and stepped right into heaven. But he said, 'Before the wedding there is one thing I should like to do, if you, my king, will give me your gracious permission.'

The king said, 'Anything, anything; you shall do anything you like!'

So what *did* Jon do? He went to the wild beast den, opened the iron doors, and said, 'Now, my beasts, come out and follow me.'

And they came out, a great procession of them, the lions leading, and then the tigers, and then the bears, and then the wolves. And Jon led them away and away into a great forest. And there, as they gathered round him in a circle, he said, 'Now, my beasts, you have your freedom; live here and be happy. But don't you ever come back bothering the king's people. Come, give me your promise!'

And the oldest lion spoke up for them all, and said, 'For your sake, Jon, we promise.'

Well, they kept their promise, and ever after lived happily in the forest. And Jon and his two brothers lived happily in the palace. Jon married the princess, and his two brothers married two ladies-in-waiting who were the princess's particular friends. And by and by, when the old king died, Jon became king, and a good king he made.

So now goodbye to you, Jon, for that's the end of the story.

10 · Bull's Winter House

Once upon a time Bull, Ram, Pig, Cat, and Cock went on their travels together. They came into a forest, and there they spent the summer very happily. They found plenty of food. Bull and Ram ate grass. Cat caught mice. Cock picked up insects and plant seeds. Pig ate up anything and everything.

Then came autumn; the wind blew and the rain fell. Bull said to Ram, 'Brother Ram, after autumn comes winter, and with winter comes snow and ice. It will be very cold – cold enough to freeze us. Come, let us build a house together.'

But Ram said, '*I* shan't freeze! I have a thick woolly coat. I shall run about and jump about and keep warm. Why should I help you to build a house?'

So Bull went to Pig. 'Brother Pig, winter is coming with snow and ice. Let us build a house together, lest we freeze.'

But Pig said, 'No, I'm not going to build a house. I shall dig a deep hole in the ground. When the snow comes I shall hide away in my hole and wait for summer.'

So Bull went to Cock. 'Brother Cock, let us build a house to live in when winter comes.'

But Cock said, 'What do I want with a house? When winter comes I shall perch in a holly tree. The berries will feed me, the leaves will shelter me. Oh, I shall be snug enough!'

So Bull went to Cat. 'Brother Cat, winter is coming. Let us build a house together, lest we freeze.'

But Cat said, 'Bother your house! I know how to keep warm. I shall curl up under Cock's holly tree, and wrap my tail round my nose.'

No, not one of them would help Bull to build a house. So he

had to build it all by himself. He chose a dry place, he got logs, he built up walls, he made a roof, he stuffed the chinks between the logs with moss, he went to town and bought a stove and a lot of food, he gathered a great pile of firewood. He worked hard: when winter came the house was finished. Bull went into the house, shut the door, and made a roaring fire in the stove.

Outside the wind was wailing, the snow was falling, and all the trees were white. But Bull sat by his fire; he was warm and cosy.

In the forest Ram was running here, running there, shaking the snow off his woolly coat. But as fast as he shook snow off his coat, so more snow fell on to it. The snow was in his eyes, in his nose, in his mouth, his horns were white with it, his woolly coat couldn't keep him warm; he ran to Bull's house and banged on the door.

'Bull, Bull, let me in, before I freeze to death!'

Bull opened the door, just a crack. *Whe-ew!* In rushed the wind, in whirled the snow. 'Brother Ram, what's this? You said you were going to run about and keep warm in your woolly coat. No, I won't let you into my house, because you wouldn't help me to build it.'

'Then I shall die – I shall die on your doorstep!'

'O, well – come in!'

Bull flung the door wide. Ram ran in and lay down by the fire. Bull slammed the door, and the wind went on its way, whirling the clouds of falling snow up and down, and round and round.

Pig had dug a hole in the ground and crept into it. But the snow was blocking up the mouth of the hole. Pig was shovelling the snow away with his snout; but as he shovelled one heap away, another heap piled up. Pig was gasping and wheezing. 'I shall be suffocated in here very soon!' he thought. And he struggled out of the hole, and ran squealing to Bull's house.

'Bull, Bull, let me in before I die!'

Bull opened the door, just a crack. 'What, Brother Pig! I thought you wanted to spend the winter lying in a hole! No, I won't let you into my house, because you didn't help to build it.'

'Then I must lie down and die on your doorstep!'

'Oh well, come in quickly!'

Bull opened the door wider. Pig staggered in, and lay down in front of the fire, beside Ram. Bull slammed the door, and brushed the snow off Pig's bristly back. 'My floor will be in a puddle soon!' said Bull.

Cock sat perched in a holly tree. The outside branches of the tree were heavy with snow, and the wind tossed them up and down, and this way and that way. Icicles hung from the inside branches, and tinkled as the wind blew. An icicle hung from each of Cock's yellow feet. His feet were numb, he couldn't hold on to the frozen branch. He tumbled head over heels out of the holly tree, pecked the icicles off his feet, and ran to Bull's house.

'Bull, Bull, let me in!'

'Oh, go away, Brother Cock! Why aren't you sitting safe and snug in your holly tree?'

'It *wasn't* safe! It *wasn't* snug!'

'Well, you wouldn't help me build my house. So why should I let you in?'

'If you don't let me in, I shall die here on your doorstep!'

'Oh well, come in!'

Bull opened the door a crack. Cock rushed in, and lay down in front of the fire beside Ram and Pig.

Cat was crouched under Cock's holly tree. He had his tail wrapped over his nose, but he couldn't keep warm. The ground was frozen hard, and the wind-blown snow was driving in under the tree. Soon Cat would be buried in it. He gave a leap, scattered the snow, and ran yowling to Bull's house.

'Bull, Bull, open the door! Let me in!'

'What, Brother Cat, is that you? Go and keep warm with your tail over your nose – you who wouldn't help me build my house! No, I won't open the door.'

'Then I shall die on your doorstep!'

'Oh well, come in!'

Bull opened the door, Cat leaped inside. Bull slammed the door, Cat clambered on to the top of the stove, and lay there shivering.

Bull piled wood on the fire. He was really kind. He had a barrel of ale in his house, and plenty of food. He handed round the food: meat for Cat, nuts and potatoes for Pig, corn for Cock, hay and bread for Ram and himself, ale for everybody. They ate, they drank, they were warm and happy.

Night came. Bull damped down the fire. They settled themselves to sleep: Cat on the stove; Pig on the hearth; Ram in one corner; Bull in another corner; Cock on a beam. . . .

Out in the forest, deep in the snow, seven hungry wolves were running and howling. They saw a tiny red flicker of light among the trees. What could it be? They came bounding. A little house! Perhaps something to eat in the house? But then, perhaps danger! They prowl around the house in the dark, sniffing and licking their lips. 'Shall we venture in? Or shall we not? Well, let one of us go in, and see how the land lies . . .! Yes, but which one . . .? Gritty Grey is the youngest of us, and the swiftest on his feet – let him go in!'

Gritty Grey doesn't much like the idea. But it is six to one; he must do as he's told. They hustle him to the door; he opens it, and creeps in. . . .

What happens?

Bull leaps up, catches Gritty Grey on his horns, and tosses him across to Ram. Ram leaps up, catches him on *his* horns, and tosses him back to Bull. Cat leaps down from the stove and claws his face. Pig leaps up and catches him by the tail. Cock runs along the beam, cackling and crowing, 'Chuck him up he-ere! I'll tear him in two-oo!' Bull catches him on his horns again, and tosses him against the door. The door flies open. Gritty Grey rushes out, he gallops away over the snow among the trees, and the six other wolves go galloping after him.

By and by they all sit down, panting.

'What happened, Gritty, what happened?'

'Oh terrible, terrible things!' cried Gritty Grey. 'Scarcely had I got inside the door when a man with a pitchfork tossed me against the wall, where there was another man with a pitchfork who tossed me in front of the stove, where an old woman sat sewing – at least I *think* it was an old woman, but I couldn't really

see – but whoever it was, thrust pins and needles into my face and nearly scratched my eyes out! And then the Devil himself came stamping across the floor and caught me by the tail; and all the time a little imp sat up on a beam shrieking "Chuck him up he-ere, and I'll tear him in two-oo!" And then the first man with the pitchfork gave me another toss to fling me up to the imp; but I fell against the door, and the door flew open – and that saved my life! But oh, oh, it was touch and go!' panted Gritty Grey. 'And catch me ever going near that house again!'

'Catch any of us going near it!' cried the other six wolves.

And they scuttled away farther into the forest, kicking up the snow with their rushing feet.

So, after that, Bull, and Ram, and Pig, and Cock, and Cat spent a peaceful winter, keeping warm in Bull's house, and gobbling up all Bull's store of food.

He was a good-natured old fellow, was Bull.

II · *Elsa and the Bear*

There was once a forester who had a wife and an only daughter called Elsa. He also had a little white poodle; and this little poodle always ran out of the house to meet him when he came home each day from his work in the king's forest.

Well now, one afternoon the forester had ridden a long way into the forest, and he came to a place that was quite unknown to him. In fact, he had ridden right over the border of the king's forest into another forest; and he was just about to turn back when he saw a nut tree whose branches were bowed almost to the ground with a heavy weight of yellow nuts as big as lemons. So he thought no harm in picking two of those nuts to carry home, one for his wife, and one for Elsa.

So there he is, down from his horse, and picking two nuts, and putting them one in each pocket.

He was just about to get on his horse again, when there came from behind the tree a roaring and a growling, and a huge black Bear leaped out upon him.

'How dare you pick my nuts!' roared the Bear.

The forester was a brave man, and quick-witted. He said to himself, 'If you can speak, my good fellow, you're no bear! You must be some great wizard or sorcerer in disguise.' So he answered as politely as he knew how, 'Gracious lord, I am the king's forester; but it seems I have strayed beyond my beat. I saw this tree and was astonished. Never before have I beheld such great and beautiful nuts.'

'But you had no right to pick them,' growled the Bear. 'Why did you pick them?'

'Gracious lord, I picked but two, to carry home and show to my wife and daughter, that they might marvel at them, even as I marvel. I will gladly pay for them, if you will name a price.'

The Bear said, 'I have no need of money. My price is what first comes running to meet you on your return home today. I will come with a carriage tomorrow and fetch my price. Is that agreed? Or shall I here and now hug you to death?'

'It is agreed, gracious lord,' said the forester. But he thought, 'Ah, my dear little white poodle, you who always run to meet me so joyously when I come home, must I then give you to the Bear? Yet better I should lose you, than that I should leave my wife a widow, and my daughter fatherless!'

So, with a heavy heart, the forester got on his horse and rode off. It was some time before he found his way out of the strange forest; but at last he came into the road that led towards home. He set his horse at a gallop. Now he could see his wife standing in the doorway; now he should have seen the little white poodle scampering to meet him. But – alas, alas! – what *did* he see? He saw his dear daughter, Elsa, running joyfully towards him, with the little white poodle in her arms.

He reined in his horse, he jumped from the saddle. Elsa tiptoed to kiss him. 'Father,' said she, 'why do you look so sad? Isn't it right that I should come to meet you?'

'No, not today. Oh, not today, my darling! But come, let us go in.'

So they walked together to the house, he leading the horse, Elsa with her arm through his, and the little white poodle trotting behind.

A stable boy was waiting to take the horse. The forester and Elsa went indoors. He had one nut in either pocket; they were so heavy, so heavy, they seemed to be weighing him down. He took them out of his pocket – what were they now? Two great lumps of glittering gold!

'One for you, my wife,' says he. 'And one for you, my little daughter.'

Ah, how they exclaimed, how they clapped their hands and jumped for joy! But the forester laid his arm on the table, and his head on his arm, and groaned. And groaning, he told them all that had happened.

'Well then,' says his wife, 'no need to grieve! We'll dress up the servant girl, and let *her* go. How should a bear know the difference between one girl and another girl?'

Elsa said, 'Oh no, we can't do that!'

Her mother said, 'Hold your tongue!'

The forester said, 'It's a bad business, but that will be best.'

So next morning Elsa's mother told the servant girl that she might take a holiday and go to the fair. And she dressed the girl up finely in Elsa's Sunday clothes. The girl looked smart, and was well pleased with herself. And scarcely was she dressed and ready, when they heard the rumbling of wheels outside; and there, in a cloud of dust, came a carriage drawn by two brown bears. And inside the carriage sprawled the great black Bear.

The black Bear put his head out of the carriage window. 'Is she ready?'

'Yes, ready and waiting,' said the forester. He took hold of the servant girl and pushed her, struggling and screaming, into the carriage. The carriage immediately drove off. Now nothing could be seen of it but a cloud of dust, and soon even that vanished from sight.

The forester heaved a sigh of relief; the wife laughed; but Elsa said, 'It's not right! I know it's not right!'

Inside the carriage the servant girl was shaking with sobs. The great black Bear laid his head on her lap and said:

> *'Tickle me, scratch me*
> *Softly and tenderly,*
> *Or else I will eat you,*
> *Skin, bone and all!'*

'Get away! Get away, you ugly beast!' shrieked the servant girl. She flung the carriage door open, jumped out, and ran to hide in the bushes by the roadside.

'Pah!' said the Bear. 'You're not the right one!'

And he drove back to the forester's house.

There he was now, out of the carriage and up on his hind legs, banging on the door, and roaring and growling:

'If you don't keep promise true,
I'll pull the house down over you!
I'll eat up father, eat up mother,
I'll have my true bride and no other!'

'I'm coming!' cried Elsa. And before anyone could stop her, she'd run out of the house and jumped into the carriage.

Her father shouted, her mother screamed, the great black Bear scrambled back into the carriage. Away went that carriage in a cloud of dust, away and away, and was lost to sight.

Then the great black Bear laid his head on Elsa's lap and said:

'Tickle me, scratch me,
Softly and tenderly,
Or else I will eat you,
Skin, bone and all.'

'I don't believe you'll do that,' said Elsa. 'Why should you?' And she put out her hand and stroked the Bear's rough shaggy head.

'Go on stroking! Go on stroking!' said the Bear.

So Elsa went on stroking the Bear's head. And by and by he gave a great sigh, and said, 'Yes, you're the right one!'

All this time the carriage was whizzing along as if a storm wind was blowing it. It had now left the road and was crashing its way through the king's forest, bumping against trees, tearing up the ground, but ever whirling on. Right through the king's forest it went, and out of the king's forest, and into the forest that lay beyond. Then suddenly it vanished; and Elsa and the Bear were standing under the nut tree.

The Bear struck the trunk of the nut tree with his snout. The trunk opened, and they went through into a narrow passage. At the end of the passage was an iron door.

'Are you brave, maiden?' said the Bear.

'I will try to be brave,' said Elsa.

123

'Dear maiden,' said the Bear. 'All may yet be well. If you can trust me, and do exactly as I tell you to do.'

'I will trust you, and do exactly what you tell me,' said Elsa.

'Then get on my back,' said the Bear. 'Put your two arms round my neck, and clasp your hands together:

'Don't look hither,
Don't look thither;
Look before you, not behind you,
Then no evil thing shall bind you.
Keep as still as any mouse,
And bring a blessing on my house.'

Elsa did as the Bear told her. She got on his back, leaned forward and clasped her two hands together round his neck. Then the Bear touched the iron door with his snout. The door opened, and they went through into a great room. Oh, horror! That room was full of all manner of hideous little creatures: toads and snakes, bats and owls, and small gibbering monkeys. The snakes hissed, the toads crawled up Elsa's legs, the bats and owls flapped in her face, the monkeys screamed and tried to drag her off the Bear's back. Was Elsa frightened? She was! But she did as the Bear had told her. She looked neither to right nor left, she looked straight in front of her, and kept her hands clasped round the Bear's neck.

So they passed through the room and came to a second door – a silver door this one was. At the door the Bear stopped and said, 'My heart, are you still there?'

'Yes, I am still here on your back,' says Elsa.

'Keep your hands clasped together,' says the Bear. 'And remember,

'Don't look hither,
Don't look thither,
Look before you, not behind you,
Then no evil thing shall bind you.
Keep as still as any mouse,
And bring a blessing on my house.'

124

Then the Bear touched the silver door with his snout. It opened, and they went through into another great room. Oh me! If the things in the first room had been terrible, the things in this second room were worse. There were huge monsters: huge hot monsters breathing out flames; and huge cold monsters breathing out icy breaths. One moment Elsa seemed to be all on fire, the next moment she seemed to be freezing to death. Ah, how terrified she was! But she did as the Bear had told her. She looked neither to right nor left; she looked straight forward, and kept her hands clasped round the Bear's neck. And so, just as she thought she could endure the torment no longer but must surely die, the Bear had crossed the room and stood before a third door – a door of glittering gold.

'My heart, are you still there?'

'Yes, I am still here on your back,' whispered Elsa.

The Bear pushed open the golden door. He gave a leap, he shook Elsa off his back. She crouched, almost fainting, with her hands before her face. There was a flash of lightning, a clap of thunder, then silence. And then a voice saying,

'Now *look hither*,
Now *look thither*,
Look before you,
Look behind you,
Evil spells no more shall bind you.
See, my darling, see, see
How all my house now blesses thee!'

Someone raised Elsa to her feet. Where was she now? Standing in a beautiful room, surrounded by a crowd of gallant lads and laughing maidens; and, best of all, clasped in the arms of a handsome prince.

'Elsa, dear Elsa,' said the prince. 'I am your Bear whom you have delivered from the vile spell of a sorcerer. These lads are my faithful companions, whom the sorcerer turned into the horrible creatures that sought to torment you. These maidens are those who failed in the task that you have so bravely accomplished. I carried them through the rooms, but they looked hither, they looked thither, they fell through the floor and lay as dead, awaiting their deliverer. Elsa, dear Elsa, will you be my wife?'

'Yes, I will be your wife,' said Elsa.

Then all the maidens clapped their hands, and all the youths shouted *Hurrah*! Outside, the forest disappeared, and where the forest had been there were towns and villages and farms and fields, with the prince's palace shining above all. The prince sent a golden coach to fetch Elsa's father and mother to the palace. They came in their best clothes, and the little white poodle came with them. Elsa was married to her handsome prince; the gallant lads each chose one of the laughing maidens for his bride. There were weddings and weddings and more weddings, and rejoicings beyond telling. They sang, they danced; the little white poodle got up on his hind legs, and danced with the best of them.

Everyone was happy. And may we be happy also!